small stations fiction

Anxos Sumai

That's How Whales Are Born

Published in 2017 by
SMALL STATIONS PRESS
20 Dimitar Manov Street, 1408 Sofia, Bulgaria
You can order books and contact the publisher at
www.smallstations.com

This book was first published in the Galician language as *Así nacen as baleas* by Editorial Galaxia (Vigo, 2007). A list of our fiction titles can be found at www.smallstations.com/fiction

This work received a grant from the General Secretariat of Culture of the Ministry of Culture, Education and University Planning of the Xunta de Galicia in the call for translation grants of the year 2016

Esta obra recibiu unha axuda da Secretaría Xeral de Cultura da Consellería de Cultura, Educación e Ordenación Universitaria da Xunta de Galicia na convocatoria de axudas para a tradución do ano 2016

ISBN 978-954-384-073-1

**Anxos
Sumai**

That's
How
Whales
Are Born

Translated from Galician by **Carys Evans-Corrales**

Small Stations Press

To Manuel Serrat Crespo for Maruyme
To Garusia Maruyme for Manuel

I didn't know then
that your blood congealed
in the earth beneath my nails
that I owed you
the budding spikes I too
harbor under my nails
the dregs of your ink
that I would finally usurp your name

I didn't know that it was you who raised me
against yourself

Marilar Aleixandre

I

MOTHER WRITES A LETTER

I think beauty is not a substance in and of itself but merely a shadow drawing, a game of chiaroscuros produced by the interplay of diverse substances.

Junichiro Tanizaki

NEEDLE

Starlings, crickets, white noise, a vowel choosing to shoot out of a phrase and shatter against the whitewashed walls and the clay tiles. Sounds. The sky like a sheet. When I'm left on the terrace and open my eyes the sky never stops moving. I try to grasp it, but it's impossible. I distract myself with a fly, with the distant barking of a dog – bow-wow – with the delicate movement of the plants Felisa cultivates on the terrace. Nothing stops: it must be because of time, which hides mischievously inside of things. Restless time.

What can it be, I wonder, that terrifies me and makes me laugh? That sound that reaches only me, that stirs me up and turns me into a wolf, searching, searching everywhere with my ears cocked? The others don't hear it – I know because it still hasn't bothered them. But it could also be that they're already used to it, used to that sound that arises beyond the street, climbs over walls, drills through the legs of the table and crawls along the swollen veins on Felisa's legs. I don't know what it is. It's a weak throb, or two metal balls rubbing together. Sometimes I find it soothing, at others, disquieting. When Felisa sits down to her embroidery I can sometimes hear the broken sound of the needle as it pierces the satin fabric, or the wounded 'ah!' of the silk when the needle passes through it with the gentle impulse of the embroiderer's finger. Later, embroidery threads slide peacefully down the fabric, creating a long, monotonous phrase, ceasing to be innocuous fibers and becoming a magnificent work of embroidery. It pleases the thread to pass through the needle's eye, allowing itself to be led by it, the great guide, the leveler of virgin paths, to then come to rest in the beautiful circumstance of being the petal of a flower, the wing of a bird, a link in the double hemstitch of a tablecloth.

Thanks to Felisa's skill, the humdrum thread that winds around the belly of a wooden spool is converted into beauty.

Mother and Father were married in 1970. Few photos are left of that wedding – only the ones that Mother hoped to preserve remained where she had left them: in a box, in a cabinet, in a dining room almost always in shadow. Mother looks elated in these photographs, with a bright smile and a joyful look in her eye. Father, handsome but serious, seems distant, aware of something that was not actually taking place at that moment. I think I remember the day when Mother tore up the rest of the photos. I was still very young and lacked the exact words to ask her why she was ripping herself up like that. I was also unable to intuit the meaning of the wrath and misery they held for her.

She was sitting on the dining-room floor. The lacquered, wooden Chinese credenza that Father had brought from one of his journeys had its doors and drawers open. Sadly and tearfully, Mother set about destroying letters and photographs. Small piles of onion-skin paper had appeared, and fragments of torn bodies were now piling up on the carpet. Father's anatomy was especially savaged. Next to him, and within reach of her hand as if to ensure their protection, she was placing the photographs and letters she had decided to keep. The letters would later be kept in her bedroom dresser along with her underwear, but the photographs would be trapped inside a box in the Chinese credenza, in the dining room nearly always in shadow.

I don't know where I'd emerged from, perhaps from a walk with my nanny Felisa, or why I went into the dining room. I only remember my mother engaging in that painful purging of memories, tearing the delicate lacework from which memory is woven. It was as if she were obliterating the lines drawn on the map of a territory whose route back to sanity was too hazardous to forget. Even so, I'm aware that the photos she would remember most were precisely those she had destroyed, and the words that would torment her most – and which she would try to shoo away with an involuntary gesture of the hand as though waving off mosquitoes – would be precisely the ones she would pretend had never been spoken or written down. I don't remember what I did after that or why I did it. It had fallen to me to be there at that exact moment, to see and record in my mind the image of my mother ripping herself up.

Or trying to put herself back together again.

As time went by, that memory served to awaken my curiosity and a desire to rebuild Mother's sentimental biography. I never managed to do it, I was never on sufficiently familiar terms with her, or to ask my uncle and aunt. Furthermore, the continuous struggle I had experienced with my mother since childhood dissuaded me from displaying the least interest in her, although the memory of that afternoon in the dining room would help me look back on her with a certain indulgence.

It's also true that I'm prone to forgetting things too quickly. I think I'm only interested in questions. Answers, when I'm faced with them, are boring. In the end I was content with the reality offered by the fiction I had crafted in order to understand certain behaviors that would help me survive and to understand my family. However, my family was limited to a small group: Uncle Cándido, Aunt Natalia and Miss Felisa. And also Ramón. Like an idiot, I have always spoken of Ramón in the present tense, but he was already gone the day I found Mother sitting amid the shadows of the dining room. Had Ramón been present at that moment, things would have been completely different, because Mother would not have been so distressed or so enraged.

Ramón liked to rummage about inside that Chinese credenza and show me the bunches of letters tied with silk ribbons according to the year in which they were written. We also rummaged through the box of photographs. In the dark, odorous nook of the Chinese credenza, Mother would also hide bars of perfumed soap, boxes of delectable chocolates, and the satin and velvet cases that held the few jewels that had belonged to my grandmother. Ramón scorned the letters in which he recognized Father's handwriting, and ignored those photos of Father regarding us through his lovely blue, ever-absent eyes. He would grumble at the sight of that man forcing a smile at us from places we didn't know, among people we'd never seen, and even accompanied by women with exotic features and long, black, straight hair. Ramón was not fond of those photos or those letters.

Neither was Mother, apparently.

Aunt Natalia, so tall, so slender, and as elegant as I remembered her, was waiting for me at the airport. In spite of having just turned sixty, she insisted on keeping up a youthful look, wearing tight-fitting clothes and shoulder-length blonde hair with white highlights. She blew me a disconcerted but effusive kiss when she recognized me from the other side of the glass door as I waited for my luggage. I returned her greeting. When I reached her, she gave me a hug and tried to take charge of my small wheeled suitcase.

'Is this all you've brought?' she asked, disappointed.

'Yes, and the backpack.'

She didn't bother looking at the backpack I carried on my shoulders, which was probably not a pleasant sight to her exquisite eyes. I also realized that my appearance repelled her somewhat. It was summer, I was wearing faded blue jeans, a sleeveless T-shirt and black leather sandals. And no, I wasn't wearing make-up or salon-styled hair. She tried to apologize for me: you look tired, it's been a long trip, college students don't worry about their looks. 'Maybe that's it,' I thought, taking her by the hand as I did when I was little and would walk at her side.

All I wanted was for her to calm down. She was nervous. We hadn't seen each other for about three years – I had left the city in June of 2004 and it was now early July of 2007. I must confess that I too found it strange to return to the city, to return home. To face Mother again. Natalia squeezed my hand, taking it to her lips to kiss. I liked that gesture. It made me feel protected.

'You relax, child. It's all right.' In the end, it was she who tried to calm me down.

I believe I've only ever done two good things for Mother. One of them was leaving home when she asked me to. She asked me on the day I turned nineteen. Her gift was a monthly allowance of fifteen hundred euros that I would receive on condition that I found a place to live when the term was over. My aunt and uncle took umbrage at this drastic decision and immediately offered to take me in. But I had already made my own plans: I was studying marine biology, I had the best academic record in my class and a desperate ambition to go somewhere to study gray whales as far away from Mother and as close as possible to fulfilling my own desires. I once loved someone whose heart weighed at least four hundred kilos, a headstrong type who was bent on finding a way to turn into a whale. He would tell me, 'Whales sing, whales breathe underwater through their lungs, whales shoot milk from their teats into the mouths of their children, who are born through their mothers' tails.' I knew hardly more than that about whales when I began to study them. Mother also loved that half-liquid, half-gaseous being who was as solid as the supports of a building, maddened by an imagination unable to distinguish between the real and the fanciful, and with an immense heart that knew only how to love my mother and how to love me: Ramón. The loss of Ramón was, I'm sure, the greatest pain Mother ever felt. Losing me, on the other hand, was the greatest relief for Mother's greatest pain. Coming home at that moment, when she was so ill, was, in Aunt Natalia's opinion, the second good thing I would do for her.

Or for myself. I wasn't exactly sure.

Aunt Natalia – an enormous, pale, strawberry smile – thanked me as we sat down in the car, taking my face in both hands and squeezing me as if I were still a baby. She pinched my cheeks and recommended a moisturizing skin cream, making apologies for me yet again: 'Your skin is dehydrated. You spend all day in salt water and under that Mexican sun that causes even the fishes to shrivel.' She made me laugh. I told her I was only a student, that I attended classes, collaborated with a whale-watching group, and took turns working in a huge aquarium where dolphins were raised in captivity. Aunt Natalia searched her handbag for a pack of cigarettes.

'But you know how to scuba-dive, don't you?'

'You bet!'

I don't know why the fact I that could scuba-dive delighted my aunt so much. Perhaps she sensed an astonishing freedom in being able to move underwater with oxygen tanks strapped to one's back. She put the car in gear and I was glad she was keeping silent as we drove along the road leading to the city. I was paying attention. On the plane I'd been overcome more than once by the fear of losing heart and turning back, but that didn't happen. I let myself be led by Natalia and realized that the years away had left a shield on my skin like a sort of nostalgia-proof raincoat. I could see, but not feel. Images entered my eyes and slid down to my feet. I sensed that at any moment my feet would start to squirm uncomfortably, as though walking over steel nails or iron tips. For the time being, all was going well: I didn't want to feel anything and felt nothing. When we were about to enter the city, I turned to Aunt Natalia and asked if She knew. If She knew I was coming home.

'But Child, it's only your mother!' There was a certain annoyance in her words, as if she were tired of repeating them. And in fact she was. She had acted as a go-between a thousand times for Mother and me when I was still a baby, then a girl, and later an adolescent and after that a college student. And then, after I'd left, she phoned me at least twice a week to chat about Mother and the family and to see how I was doing. In those days I would think of her tenderly, trying to latch onto her strength. I remembered the day she called me – barely a month ago – to ask me to return. I was on the beach drinking tequila with Kazuo, a Japanese man who had just arrived at the Bay. Angela was also there, a professor from the Canary Islands who did research on jellyfish for the University of California.

My aunt's voice had become familiar in every space I'd occupied since my mother asked me to leave home. It accompanied me everywhere like my most beloved books, the faded, old Kent Miller marine action figure that had belonged to my brother, and a short, concise photo album. The old soldier was missing a leg, my books had become a little more tattered with each journey, and the photo album had also increased with each trip, but Natalia's voice remained the same: bouncy and musical, sometimes unstable, and it was even possible to tell from its tone the color of the sky on the other end of the line. But when she phoned me a month ago her voice was deep, as though dressed in a heavy woolen coat. I sensed that a heavy zinc-gray sky weighed over the city. It was the very same sober voice in which she had told me, two years previously, that Mother had taken the unquestionable decision to lock herself up in her room forever. Mother tends to take terribly drastic decisions which absolutely cannot be questioned. It was hard for her to decide. It was very difficult for her to come to a decision; she would meditate, study all possible outcomes in the utmost secrecy, and finally utter a few words, and the Earth would change its trajectory. She made one of these decisions when, in view of Uncle Cándido's passivity at the helm of the hardware store, she decided to expand the family business and set up an electrical appliances establishment, which, in time, would grow into a chain specializing in household goods: furniture, carpets, bed linen, crockery, sugar bowls with flies caught in their lids, chairs that imitated the painful seats of one's grandparents' homes, Italian towels, Indian blankets, and reproductions of African statuary. But between those decisions that would turn her into a brilliantly successful entrepreneur, Mother could sometimes become a monster when it came to other decisions, and would at other times transform into a completely depressive and defenseless creature. When she sank into these impenetrable, inconsolable states, Aunt Natalia and I would say – somewhat cruelly – that she was 'caught in the centrifuge.' The very thought of Mother caught in a centrifuge made us laugh, made us feel like accomplices, and this saved us from lapsing into depression. These were truly intolerable times for the entire family.

Mother had just turned fifty-five when she decided to lock herself up in her bedroom. The stores had been functioning for a long time without her assistance and were doing well – very well. It was time for her to fall into one of those agonizing maelstroms, because this is how it had been throughout her life. When she locked herself into her room she was defeated, yearning to be transported to some place where destiny would be waiting for her. It didn't matter where: Mother always needed a destiny to set herself into action, to relinquish the voluntary self-exile she would impose on herself when neither death nor her loved ones could move her at all.

I looked for questions to inspire enthusiasm in life, but she was in desperate need of a mission, a specific, precise obligation, something that would give meaning to the ten fingers on her hands, the joints of her bones, and the tenderness that at some point would take shape inside her. Here, in life, it seemed to have been years since she'd last found it. I imagine when Mother shut herself in her room, she had already spent time undoing the lacework of memory she had taken so long to create, and that day when I found her sitting in the shadows of the dining room, she was starting to come undone, unweaving and erasing the paths that could bring her back. I think it was a totally voluntary act, like those suicides who decide to kill themselves not during their greatest suffering, but during flashes of lucidity. But things were already happening before she tore Father to pieces as she sat on the dining room floor. The loss of her destiny, for example, had already occurred.

Mother was born to take care of her parents; and her parents died – when she was still an adolescent – in a terrible fire that razed the family hardware store. She felt lost, as she'd been raised to think that her life would only have meaning if it was devoted to the care of some elderly parents, a responsibility to be incumbent upon her when the time came. Her parents had first had a son, Cándido, to whom they would leave the business. Mother and Uncle Cándido were born with their fates laid out before them. My uncle Cándido took possession of his when he was twenty years old, after the fire, and had to lift the family out of the ashes with very little experience. It seemed to him a huge injustice to have to surrender his youth to the reconstruction of a hardware store reduced to iron, smoke, and mud. But this is what he'd been born for, wasn't it? Working day and night in the damned store, all he needed was to find someone on whom he could vent his frustration. And he found Aunt Natalia.

He found her the day she came in to buy a porcelain coffee pot.

'Now why do we call a piece of enameled metal *porcelain*?' Uncle Cándido would ask himself such questions when faced with the chipped crockery Mother had insisted on using for years in the kitchen. It hurt, as it reminded him of his lost youth.

'Because of the enamel, which imitates fine porcelain – the real kind,' Aunt Natalia would patiently explain.

'The poor man's porcelain for eating worm-ridden lentils!' Uncle Cándido would rage. 'That's what we've always been: poverty-stricken wretches. Why didn't I sail off somewhere, like everybody else?'

I remember those words that Uncle Cándido would threaten us with when he was angry. Even knowing we were in fact a rich family – thanks to Mother's decisions – Uncle Cándido could only see an ancient poverty that arose not from a lack of money but from a lack of dreams. And he saw his 'Why didn't I sail off somewhere like everybody else?' (aimed at Mother, and incidentally also at Aunt Natalia, who thought that being his wife would be enough to make my uncle happy) as the greatest insult he could possibly hurl at them. Thanks to an inexplicable empathy, Aunt Natalia felt the same way as Mother during extreme circumstances, despite their not being able to stand one another. The mere mention of 'sailing off somewhere,' especially if coming from Uncle Cándido, became a direct attack on both of them. But that's another story.

Uncle Cándido wasn't in the least satisfied with his lot in life, but had accepted it without rebellion or ambition as one more link in the history of that establishment, now a century old. Even his name, a name bestowed upon all the family's firstborn males, had been tied around his neck in the same way as a gold medallion of Our Lady of Carmel had been. I think it was on account of Uncle Cándido's name that my grandmother and her family ultimately stopped talking to each other. In fact, neither Mother nor my uncle ever mentioned those relatives, other than to deride them for their vanity and arrogance. I've sometimes run into people who've told me I was just like my maternal grandmother and that what happened was a crying shame.

At one point I went out with a fellow who shared my mother's rather uncommon surname. When we realized we were second cousins, we felt so revolted that we no longer had the least intention to continue seeing each other again. When I was a student in the city, I would come across him in the mornings on my way to the university. We wouldn't even exchange greetings, but I was sure we looked at each other out of the corner of our eyes. (I admit that I did.) He walked upright, stiff, wearing a suit and tie. He carried an umbrella when it rained, an enormous, black, good-quality umbrella, and his boots resounded as their soles struck the flagstones. When it wasn't raining, he still wore a suit and tie but didn't carry an umbrella, and his shoes were made of soft black or brown leather, matching his clothes. His life didn't seem much different to me from Uncle Cándido's;

they were both dispassionate, unconscious duplicators of the same daily rituals, unaware that life was a huge project that existed beyond the scope of both of them. In spite of them.

I think that fellow and I, without any need to exchange glances, had noticed the backpacks we were carrying and realized those burdens weren't our own. But even with this awareness, and in spite of recognizing a certain common misfortune in both of us, we continued to keep our distance. I remember that the only thing I could think of to say to him as our paths crossed was, 'We're innocent,' but I'd say it voicelessly, swallowing the disdain of his haughty nose – which was just like mine – and the angles that would soon encourage his passion and, therefore, a certain degree of beauty into my life.

When Uncle Cándido turned five, my grandparents realized it was time to create a daughter that would look after them in their old age. They were in luck yet again. Grandmother gave birth to a girl. Mother's destiny seemed even more horrifying than Uncle Cándido's: he was to take possession of the business, whereas she would be raised and constrained never to forget that she had been born with the purpose of looking after her parents.

They received a similar education. They studied at the same grade school and at the same secondary school. One after the other, they read the same books that formed part of the family library, and were supplied with selections of abridged classics from *Readers Digest* and the *Círculo de Lectores* catalog. They saw the same movies and interacted only with the neighborhood children. Both were smart and curious; they could have made anything they wanted out of their futures, had they not been constantly cautioned that they'd been born for a purpose. I suppose both of them dreamed of running away from home and seeking refuge in that other part of the family they didn't get along with, and they did it with the same furious, futile imagination as when they dreamed of being the offspring of a superhero who would fly to deliver them of their childhood woes.

As soon as he was done with high school, Uncle Cándido began to work at the hardware store. He was a good student, but the possibility of rebelling and breaking the chain didn't even cross his mind. He couldn't do it. Nailed to his body was the same iron-lettered name that had clung for years to the door's lintel: 'Cándido Hardware, Inc.' Mother was still at school when the fire occurred. She was fifteen years old, a teenager with long blonde hair. After high school she attended a dressmaking academy, because Grandmother knew full well that any woman whose fate involved the care of very elderly parents needed to have a basic knowledge of sewing, embroidery, and – since this already existed – tinting and styling hair. She would learn other essentials by herself, on the spot, instantly, when it was necessary for her to take action.

The fire left her stunned, paralyzed in the face of the future and unable to react. Rather than feeling released, she decided to find someone to whom she could turn over the ten fingers on her hands, the joints of her bones, and the tenderness that at some remote moment had solidified in the cells of her womb.

One day, many years ago now, seated behind the counter and with his head in his hands, Matías, the porter, tried to find an explanation as to how an enormous papier-mâché whale had reached the building. He hadn't seen anyone come in with such a thing. He became convinced that he was already too old for such surprises. 'Whoever brought it will return for it,' he told himself, devoting himself to arranging the mail for delivery to the respective floors in the afternoon. He never used the elevator, and it became increasingly hard for him to go up the stairs, but it was an exercise imposed upon him at least once a day: going up and down the stairs.

'Who would want such a horrible thing?' he wondered from the first step, looking at the animal's back from above.

He continued up the stairs with the feeling that the whale reminded him of someone. When he rang the bell on our floor, he slapped his hand to his forehead and exclaimed:

'Ramón!'

When he came downstairs to the entrance, he faced the great whale once more, tenderly caressing its head and leaning forward to look into its eyes. He even found it beautiful.

Sorrowfully beautiful, like Ramón's ridiculous happiness.

Solicitously, Matías opened the door and tried to give me hug. He was a nervous man, as thin as a dancer, and so elderly that I was ashamed to let him carry my wheeled suitcase. Hurt, he insisted, and I ended up agreeing to it.

'The Child's back! The Child's here!' he exclaimed, moving his head non-stop from side to side and always about to burst into a guffaw. 'The Child! I still remember that horrific animal you brought into my building.'

'And what a fright that gave you! Do you really remember that?'

Aunt Natalia pressed the elevator button while Matías and I spoke at the gateway.

'How could I not remember? I even remember the day you were born!'

He shook his head, looked at the floor, looked at the ceiling, then looked at me. Surprised, I regarded him curiously, wondering how old this man must be who also remembered the day my Mother had been born.

'I'm truly sorry about Madam...'

He fell silent, abashed. Aunt Natalie pried the suitcase from his hand and we entered the elevator. We went up in silence. I examined each corner of the elevator car, which

I knew as well as any corner of my body. They hadn't even fixed the mirror against which I had smashed a hideous ceramic doll that Mother had given me. I wanted a Barbie and she gave me a dead doll, covered in frills and wearing a camisole. I wanted an orange-colored plastic wristwatch and she gave me a young lady's watch with a fine golden strap. I wanted nothing at all and she would slap me.

'Do you feel any calmer?' asked my aunt. I didn't answer. She took my face in her hands once again, pinched my cheeks, and, whispering into my ear in a low voice, repeated the words 'calm and relaxed.' 'She's not going to eat you. Or you her, I imagine.'

Felisa was waiting for us at the door. Matías must have informed her right away. Felisa: small, round, quick on her heels. Snooty and a bit vulgar – as always – she put her arms around me, pressing me against her breasts, which felt soft around my hips. The upper part of her head reached my neck and I could see her bald spots concealed beneath the violet-tinted hair, straightened, folded and puffed out to give volume to her few remaining strands. She flooded my T-shirt with tears and saliva, and if she hadn't been so broad and heavy, I would have grabbed her and thrown her into the air like a top. Or a kite. But she was heavy, kept gripping me, and would not stop sniveling.

Ever since I stopped living in that apartment, I always found my encounters with Felisa to be fearsome. No matter where I was, she would stick to me like a limpet and there would be no way of escaping her embrace.

When I was little, the one who really took care of me was Ramón. When he went off to work at the hardware store, Ramón would leave me in the penthouse with Felisa. It happened one day after lunch, at siesta time. Felisa had put me to bed, covered by a light summer blanket. The bedroom window was open, veiled by a linen curtain that she herself had embroidered. But it was summertime, four o'clock in the afternoon, and the curtain wasn't sufficient to keep out the light, so before lying down beside me and starting her daily lullaby session, Felisa lowered the blinds. The sunlight began to shine through the spaces between their slats, penetrating the linen and crossing through the darkness of the room. Mesmerized, I stared at the motes of dust caught in the light. They were dancing. Hoping they would disappear, I opened and shut my eyes, carried away by that interminable game: the air was alive, the light was a ribbon on which restless beings were nervously playing.

Felisa tried her best to lull me to sleep, but it was impossible: I was still entangled in that silent game played by those tiny beings populating the air. I closed my eyes and the light frolicked behind my eyelids, the dust was putting down roots in that part of the brain where memories accumulate and are always kept as fresh as in a fridge. The dust, the air, the light were playing inside me – with me. Then Felisa stroked my hair, slowly and tenderly. I felt her breathing close to me, her breath of freshly-consumed and over-sweetened coffee streaming down the nape of my neck. Later, murmuring as though telling me a story, she said:

'You'll never forget this moment, darling child. Never.'

She became quiet and seemed to fall asleep. For my part, I felt the dust-laden strip of air knotting itself in my stomach. I felt afraid. I felt fear for the first time. Fear of the silence that came after, the darkness that prevailed over the sunbeams pouring through the blinds, the cold that filled my tiny feet, chubby and bare.

And Felisa was right. I never did forget that moment. Or the smell of her breath, or the rigid, cold, sad immobility that kept her lying on the bed, looking at me as if at a wish she would never be granted.

In the same way the memory of Mother tearing up letters in a darkened room made me become indulgent, the image of Felisa looking at me like an unattainable dream helped me endure her endless embrace. I waited. Her tears seeped through my T-shirt and felt cool and salty inside my stomach. I waited, and her breasts were so jostled from weeping that my hips would quiver restlessly. I waited, and seeing her leathery scalp under the few strands of hair that held her snooty dignity together, I behaved as though a puppy had me by a hand. I stroked her neck, slowly and delicately. Slowly and waiting.

Slowly, she moved away from me, looking at me through eyes brimming with tears, with the violet eyeshadow she always wore running down toward the corners of her lips. I was unable to kiss her or give her more than a weak smile. I don't know why, but whenever I looked at Felisa the thought of an elephant would come to mind: patient but resentful. Yes, I don't know why, but there was something in Felisa's gaze that prevented me from trusting her. Beyond her abundant flesh and seemingly infinite patience, there was an accusatory look, a look that blamed me, expecting me to attack so she could then kill me. Something along those lines, but maybe I was being unfair to her, because rather than loving elephants, I sided with whales.

Once again, Aunt Natalia took on the responsibility of apologizing for me: the Child is very tired, the trip takes nearly a whole day, and we'll see her while she's here. And Felisa entered the apartment behind us, looking at me, studying me to make sure I wasn't that daughter who had never, ever, been granted her.

The house smelled of boiled vegetables, of lemon-scented cleaning products, of medicine, of moonshine. The sharp, narcotic odor of moonshine reminded me of a house I visited as a small child to see a sick friend. My friend, Lurdiñas, had leukemia. She was lying in bed, bald, with her eyes rolled back and macerating in that odor that sought to convey a categorical determination to chop the disease off at its roots. To me, death smells like moonshine and burned mango wood, but I didn't say so out loud. Aunt Natalia was so irritated that she threw my suitcase against the living-room table and nearly shattered a glass butterfly that Felisa picked up from the rug as if recovering the very essence of her being. Contrary to what I had imagined, I wasn't uneasy or nervous, I felt no fear whatsoever. I wanted to continue on to the room that had always been Mother's, but Natalia grabbed me by the arm and asked me to please wait.

It was she who went down the hallway with Felisa in tow. Finally, I was left alone. It had been five years since I'd set foot in the house, but from what I could see, everything was more or less the same. I found it strange to have to wait to be welcomed by my own mother in the house I considered my own, at the center of the small library in which I learned to live. I moved closer. I read the titles on the spines of the books and ascertained they were where they'd always been, watched over by Ramón to make sure they wouldn't escape from the strict order he'd imposed upon them. Their number had neither increased nor decreased. I looked for a book, opened it, and found within a bus ticket with a phone number. I knew it would be there, stuck to a page that preserved an impeccable image of a spider weaving its web. Just where I expected it, the spider insisted on endlessly weaving its web in blue ink. Right on that page was the bus ticket and a phone number that I would call – I'd promised myself I would – on one of those days I was in the darkened apartment, inside the luxurious building, in a city that was already less alien to me than Angela herself.

Angela was there the day Aunt Natalia had called to speak to me in that serious, dressed-up voice she only put on when very serious things had happened.

'You've got to come home, Child. Your mother's very ill.'

'What does "very ill" mean?

'It means you have to come and sign some papers.'

Ah! Signing papers. I was on the beach drinking tequila with Kazuo and Angela. It was nearly sunset, and aside from being totally drunk, I had nestled softly into my friend's geography. Our bodies had learned how to blend with each other's for three years now. I asked Natalia how long the papers could wait, and she said only a few days. I bargained with her, arguing that I was at the end of the academic year, and bought myself a month. Angela was rather startled by the scant interest I displayed in my mother. I told her that my interest in my mother was restricted to the fact that in five years my monthly allowance had increased from fifteen hundred euros to three thousand. With that money I could travel from the Bay of La Paz to San Diego whenever I missed my friend, something that happened at least once a week. Sometimes it happened every day of the week, but I was able to control the desire. So was Angela.

While I rummaged among the library shelves, waiting to be granted admittance to my mother's room, I remembered Angela's farewell at the La Paz airport, and she felt very far away, like a story that had occurred long ago, leaving behind only a memory coated in a sweet, warm, yet sticky patina. During our goodbye she had asked me to hold her, to blend into her body much as one continent may blend into another. She said, 'This is your place.' I closed my eyes and repeated, because she asked me to, insistently, 'This is my place.' But I felt that the hollow of her body into which I had fit like a nut on a bolt was becoming alien to me. It was beginning to fall apart. Whenever I left a place, it would become blurry, vanishing at the same time the new space I would occupy began taking shape, even before I'd set foot in it. People and passions, caresses and words would also become blurred along with the place. I have never been one to surrender definitively to anything. I've never been able to surrender with the safety, anxiety and perpetual desire that Angela demanded from me. To anyone. Anywhere.

The memory of Angela was completely erased when I came across the tortoiseshell-covered notebook upon which Mother had bestowed the pretentious title *Anthology of Quotidian Objects*. Mother mixed up her reading of poetry with the scrupulous examination of delivery notes, accounting ledgers and appliance catalogs, and poetry is not easily digested when mixed with nuts and wrenches and meat grinders. I suppose one of those awful indigestions gave rise to the title of the notebook, which was dedicated exclusively to Ramón. It seemed as though they were playing a game to keep Ramón's feet anchored to the ground, preventing him from flying off into delusion like a blimp or a flying whale. The game consisted of having Ramón define everyday objects that surrounded them. I opened the book and read a few definitions. I wondered what my brother must have been thinking about when he defined the word coconut: 'A coconut is like the butt of a blonde monkey, but with three holes. The coconut's holes are opened with a corkscrew or a sharp knife. Water has to come out. If no water comes out, it means the coconut is rotten.' I laughed at first, but I immediately sensed the first pang of sadness – wretched sadness – trying to possess me, and I left the notebook on the shelf. It was odd: I had lived with Ramón for three years, but he was the only person, the only thing, that hadn't been erased and for some unexpected reason inspired pain and tenderness whenever he appeared before me.

I was finally facing Mother. I watched the scene from the doorway. I found crossing the threshold hard to do. Felisa and Aunt Natalia observed my emotions, expecting me to be taken over by some atrocious sensation that would shatter the composure of my face, or cause me to throw myself, broken-hearted, into the bedridden woman's arms. They were also watching her, fearful of her first words. But she didn't utter any. Resting against large satin-covered pillows that had surely been embroidered by Felisa, Mother gave me a placid look that I found hard to recognize. I didn't know whether or not I should kiss her. I approached the bed and looked at her. She looked lovely. Her hair was gathered at the nape of her neck and her cheeks had been tinged with a light pink blush, a sign of life. She had done her eyelids with the same brown hue of her eyes and highlighted her lips with a warm pomegranate lipstick. Yes, she was truly lovely to look at. No one would have guessed she was an ailing woman were it not for how emaciated she was. 'You look beautiful.' This was the first thing that came to my mind, the first thing I was absolutely certain was entirely true. She'd always known when I was lying. She had a special skill for smelling fear in me and recognizing deceit.

She responded with a smile and I decided that kissing her on the forehead would be the best thing to do, as with any other sick person. She took my hand when I leaned over the bed. She seemed on the verge of tears, but Mother also had a special skill at concealing her emotions if she wanted to. Overcoming an old and deep-seated rejection, I stroked her head softly and timidly. Time passed slowly as her gaze traveled over my hands, arms, and face. After taking in my body, Mother gazed at the bed, gazed at the dresser, gazed at the table. She was pensive for a long time, finding it difficult to concentrate. During the process that led to her final decision, she must have gone through many irrelevant memories… you could tell from her expression that she was lost, meandering, that certain recollections were painful for her, that she was making an effort to concentrate. She finally looked into my pupils and told me something I know must not have been very easy for her to say:

'I've never hated you, Child.'

I felt a growing void in my stomach, like vertigo. It was difficult for me to reply:

'I don't hate you either, Mommy.'

From that moment on, as though pierced by a corkscrew in the right place – in one of the three holes on Ramón's coconut – emotions began to flow, landing on the bed. All the same, it wasn't easy to speak to a woman with whom communication had never before been possible. Nor was it the moment to go over our lives, it was no time for accusations or finger-pointing. It was, rather, the time to be silent, inspecting each other like a first encounter between two animals sounding out danger.

'Your aunt has made your room ready,' she said, and I knew she was asking me to stay with her. I thanked her and sat down in an armchair upholstered in yellow velvet that had been in the foyer for years. Felisa informed us with gravity that it was time for afternoon tea and that she was going to get everything ready. Natalia looked at the clock and announced that Uncle Cándido would be arriving soon.

'It must be eight o'clock already,' remarked Mother. She knew that room better than anyone. She knew the transit of the sun, the spacing of the shadows, the oscillations of the half-light. She knew exactly what time of day it was without any need to consult a clock. Her eyes followed the retreat of a sunbeam toward the quilt folded at the foot of the bed. The sunlight was playing on the turned-down sheet at the bed's head, and in a few minutes would be starting to recede to its foot.

'Ten minutes past eight,' specified Natalia.

I glanced sideways at the entire room, not yet daring to look forward, as though the room belonged to someone totally unknown to me. It was clean and tidy. I imagined she would not allow a bottle of pills or a glass of milk to be left on the nightstand. I imagined that from her bed she would still know whether or not her underwear was properly arranged inside the dresser. Or maybe she'd changed. Maybe that placid look was trying to show me she was a new, different, all-embracing woman. Everything she hadn't been before.

Before, at least prior to surrendering to voluntary seclusion, to a tedium far beyond any effort at reasoning with her, Mother would make us tremble with a single gesture when she was enraged. She would turn her back to conceal the wrath that we would later see in her face when she turned around to look at us. She wouldn't utter one damn word. She would stare at us fixedly, but it wasn't those deep brown, fiery eyes that frightened us, but her mouth. The way her mouth would become flat, betraying a remote darkness between her rows of teeth, which, in turn, attacked us from between lips that neither smiled nor displayed sadness. The darkness of that mouth was a huge amazement to us. It was also our greatest terror.

Now, in her illness, she appeared to lack the strength to express anger. I think she was even unable to feel. She only intended to breathe, eat, sleep and surrender her body to the care of alien hands. When illness turns you into a dependent being, you finally learn what it is to be humble. And while all of us might have thought that Mother's malady was basically voluntary, her mind had deteriorated, deep inside, much more than was apparent, as Natalia insisted. The poor thing had suffered so much that she hadn't been able to assimilate all the pain that had been meted out to her alone. We might say she was able to mold it into resentment and a foul temperament, a permanent victim complex that turned her into an unbearably egocentric character. Her final exhaustion and surrender had been assisted by the vast quantity of tranquilizers, analgesics and sleeping pills she'd taken, and which had drilled voids in her brain as though bored through by persistently famished woodworms.

I didn't know what her rages must have been like after her final exhaustion and decision to let herself die. I imagined that the monster we feared so greatly must be agonizing along with her, and barely had the strength to reach her mouth. When I saw her teeth, still perfect and white, they seemed so small to me that I was overcome by an enormous sense of compassion that I concealed by examining the room again. The curtains were drawn back, and in front of the window a table decorated with an embroidered cloth and a vase packed with daisies looked like a bride. On the dresser, covered by a festooned shawl, was a perfectly aligned row of silver frames showing photographs, mostly of Ramón: Ramón as a baby, Ramón at school in front of a globe of the world, Ramón dressed as a sailor for his First Communion, Ramón at the beach, Ramón in the park, Ramón in a wicker basket by the swimming pool at Aunt and Uncle's villa. Ramón blowing out candles on a giant strawberry and cream cake on his twelfth birthday. Tiny Ramón, firmly gripping the reins of a pony. There were also some photos of me, but fewer. Only the official ones from my baptism, the First

Communion, and of me receiving an award from a high-school contest. There wasn't a single photo of Father.

The room smelled of medicine, jasmine perfume, and hanging from a corner of an ancient, pirouetting calendar, from an echo on the verge of fading away, there came a warm waft of moonshine. I looked away from the dresser when I realized that Mother was watching me. I was seized by a vague shudder of guilt or shame and thought, with a start, that perhaps she had always been aware of all my intimacies.

The bell finally rang. Uncle Cándido, looking enormous, swept through the room and snatched me up from the armchair. He held me aloft, like when I was little. Mother watched us with a nostalgic air and Felisa, standing at the threshold with a tray full of tiny teacups, waited for my uncle's effusion to fade away.

'Everything's fine, everything's fine,' Natalia repeated, tall, thin and elegant, walking about the room's restricted space with her eyes resting on the delicate perfection of her nail polish.

My bedroom was presented to me under the dim lamplight looking nearly as I had left it five years ago. The bed, dressed in peach-colored sheets and pillows and covered in a fine summer quilt, invited me to yield to the desired flatness. On the old work table someone had placed a large glass vase crammed with white daisies like the ones in Mother's room. I liked the warm welcome of my bedroom, I liked seeing up on the walls the photographs of marine landscapes that accompanied me during my first years in college. At an unhurried, considered glance I could not find any alterations to the space that had been mine since birth. Only the flowers, a new pajama set folded at the foot of the bed and a clean set of towels testified to the fact that someone had entered the room in recent hours.

But I was truly surprised to see the enormous gray whale that had been a source of arguments with Mother. We had crafted it out of cardboard with a group of school friends, to use as a disguise during carnivals. It was open at the bottom and three of us could fit inside to move it around. It certainly was impressive. I was reminded of the day that we brought it to my room for safekeeping and Matías was frightened to see it at the entrance to the building. I also remember that Matías, after delivering the mail to the apartments, looked the whale in the eyes, because the eyes he saw were mine. From inside the cardboard hulk I was able to pick up, in the depth of that glassy and somewhat faded look, an enormous tenderness that made me wonder what Matías was seeing as he looked into the eyes of the fake whale that unbalanced the natural order of the building's entrance.

Well, there it was, leaning against one of the walls. Large and lovely, with peeling paint in some parts, and the eyeholes opening onto the inner void. It seemed so strange that Mother hadn't thrown it into the trash after I left. How odd. Perhaps, and in spite of her unquestionable decision, the whale was there to remind her that I still existed.

I went to bed at last and began to fall into a black and red whirlpool, which like a chute and the slight vertigo of one who slides down it, took me from lucidity to the spongy mantle of sleep. But before falling asleep altogether, an old pleasurable feeling nestled in my stomach and turned me into a baby.

I'm two years old minus one fourth. I'm a baby. I can walk and I can talk a little. I'm just short of two years old. Each year is one of my mother's breasts, and I'm eating them away in bits until I'm done. I ate her left breast the first year. Now I have less than a quarter left on the right breast to finish the second year, and I'm getting bored from eating so much. I'm not allowed to do much more than eat and sleep. I've already slept an entire turn around my belly button. I like my feet better than my belly button: I know my feet will take me very far and that the belly button will be attached to Mother's belly button, which was tied to her mother's belly button and so forth, from mother to mother. When I sleep, I fall into a black and red spiral that mixes red, living blood, with black, dead blood. I'm a baby: I'm under no obligation to know how to explain these things; I don't have enough words to retell them or experience to understand them. I know that I am safe, I float, I am tired of eating dirt out of the planters and dirt from the soil when we go to my uncle and aunt's villa and then get tummy aches. They hurt. They hurt. They worm me like a household pet so I won't get worms, that's why we babies no longer have worms in our guts. It must be very uncomfortable for a mother to have to pull living worms out of a baby's butt, among the feces. I can't imagine Mother doing such a thing. She would be very angry to have a worm writhing in her fingers. Mama does not do such things, and I don't get worms in my tummy, no matter how much dirt I eat. I have a short and chubby nanny who used to drink vinegar to lose weight when she was young and who dreamed of having a tapeworm, meters and meters long in her intestines, that would eat the food she couldn't stop gobbling. When the nanny isn't around, Ramón is in charge of changing my diapers, bathing me and rubbing my body with odorous, hydrating, calming oil. Ramón knows how to grab my feet with a single hand, folding his enormous fingers over them, and with a free hand separating my thighs to put on a clean diaper. He cleanses me with delicate and perfumed towelettes, and then sprinkles a substantial amount of talcum powder over my unripened genitals. I laugh, I let myself be caressed, I allow myself to be weak in the hands of someone who tickles my belly button with his tongue, who sings me songs and cuddles me, protecting me with his enormous chest. I feel that life is sweet, that I grow with each caress my brother unfolds over the new curves that form in my body day after day. I like his caresses, I like how he smells, I like it when he makes up lullabies for me. Some he forgets, but others stay in his mind and he often repeats them:

There's a volcano in Japan,
its name is Fujiyama.
Its hair is white
like an old Japanese.
And the Pacific Ocean
laps at its lovely feet.

Ramón likes it when I laugh. He strokes me front and back, and if he could, I'm sure he would turn me inside out like a glove and stroke my innards. When he sings, his voice is like a burst of bubbles that intoxicate me and my eyes become merry, as if a crowd of fireflies were peering through my pupils. I like being Ramón's because if they didn't worm me like a household cat, Ramón would pull the worms out of me and would show them to me, wriggling among his fingers, and we would both laugh, intoxicated by our involuntary glee.

As the morning gave way to noon I left the apartment and came across Felisa talking with Matías. They were trying to hide a passion that had gripped them for years, but I made my excuses, telling them that Aunt Natalia was waiting for me in the car. They kept on talking after Matías walked me to the entrance and closed the door behind me.

'I don't know what to tell you, Miss Felisa, but it's a shame,' said old Matías, rearing his head above his hunched body. He had always been a slight man, thin, but as he aged he became thinner and smaller. The tips on the collar of his shirt were dancing around his neck and his head bobbed constantly from side to side, up and down, like the head of a wooden turtle.

'It's a shame an old lady like you should have to take care of such a young woman.'

Miss Felisa straightened up in her high heels and sighed. Her breasts, lying over her abdomen like two placid, tired hills, perked up flirtatiously and somewhat indignantly.

'What's all this talk about old ladies?'

Matías enjoyed provoking her. He knew from her protests that Felisa enjoyed those remarks.

'I don't mean it that way, little lady. You still have some fine curves. If you're interested, my Ferrari's in tip-top shape, you can be sure of that.'

'Your Ferrari falls apart just looking at it. Never mind trying to take it for a spin!'

Matías would then burst out laughing, because he would picture her flesh untrammeled, corsetless, and picture himself naked, skinny, a wrinkled little chicken trying to possess that gorgeous enormity.

'You don't need to swear to it, Miss Felisa!' and he laughed for reasons far different from those that also had Felisa laughing, repeating over and over that they were two crazy old-timers.

'Yes, Ma'am, we're two crazy old-timers. And who cares? We don't matter anymore. I'm even useless at scrubbing stairs.'

When it seemed that he was on the verge of collapsing under the weighty hopelessness of age, Matías slammed his hand against the desk at the entrance and, stiff as a broom, began performing a few dance steps. He hummed a bolero that Felisa also knew and took her by waist, dancing for a few minutes until she pushed him away with a slap to the shoulder. She pushed him away because her legs hurt, because she was unable to keep up with the doorman's agile steps, because she was blushing and didn't want him to know about her age-old longing. She untwined from him, rearranged her skirt and the neckline of her blouse, picked up her bag in her timid hands and walked toward the elevator, muttering that they weren't children and shouldn't be engaging in such gaiety.

'We don't matter anymore, Miss Felisa,' muttered Matías, pressing the elevator button.

The wait was a joyful time for Felisa. It was a spell against not mattering any more. Salvation against nothingness. They remained quiet, looking at the ceiling. From the ceiling, piercing the building's floors, would descend the possibility of separation, and the sweet bliss of sleep, when they would think about each other after their parting. Felisa truly believed that things were fine as they were, and Matías thought that this was the best that could happen to them: meeting and separating several times a day, with nothing permanent. Mobility also delivered him from the forces of nothingness.

'I have to go upstairs. Madam's alone,' said Felisa, justifying herself as the elevator door set the separation ritual in motion. As she went up, a fistful of pins pricked her stomach. She looked at herself in the mirror, smiled, and thought she was still alive. The shade of her red lipstick still suited her.

'The Child's been crying all day long,' complained Mother from her room.

'She may have been dreaming, Ma'am,' Felisa replied, repeating in a low voice, 'Patience, patience, patience. We have a bad day coming up.' She hung up the jacket, left her handbag on the foyer table, and, looking at herself in the mirror, tidied her bangs. Before entering the room, she'd thought about what she'd say to the Señora if she mentioned the Child's weeping again. Any excuse would do, she decided, and shaped the most convincing smile she could fashion at that moment.

'The Child's gone out with Miss Natalia. They had to sign some papers,' she said with stunning certainty as she finally entered the room. Mother, sitting up in bed surrounded by large pillows, gossip magazines, a cellphone and a remote control, was watching TV. With a painful grimace she turned her head slightly when Felisa spoke. She wanted to insist that the Child had wept all day, but thought better of it and returned her attention to the screen. She was watching a movie. A woman with a knife stuck in her back was falling on her knees onto an unmade bed. The sheets appeared to be satin. They were shiny, and even on television had the rich feel of satin and its soft touch. It wasn't long before they were soaked in blood, and Mother took the remote and changed channels.

'Why should blood be red? If it were blue, it wouldn't be so unpleasant,' she remarked in annoyance. A mass of charred pigs then appeared on the screen. Some were still alive and eyed the camera, tormented by pain.

'That's outrageous!' Felisa said indignantly, turning her back on the television. Mother began to laugh.

'They're only pigs, silly!'

Felisa approached the window and drew back the curtains, which spread out to each side like a whirl of ballerinas. With a rustle of tearing tulle skirts, they gave way to the sunlight, which paused on the bed and, progressing toward the pillows, set Mother's hair afire. She was so pale that Felisa, who'd been distracted watching life on the street, felt a chill when she turned around and saw her head-on, her eyes feverish from her self-imposed torture, her red curls cascading over the white linen. An old image of a drowned girl floating in the silence of a graveyard came to Felisa's mind.

Mother changed channels again. The woman with the knife plunged into her back was being dissected by a special police forensic unit. There was no blood anymore: there was skin, flesh, bones and the stainless steel of the autopsy equipment. Felisa could still hear Matías's voice in her head and the agonized expressions of the scorched pigs.

'If blood were green or yellow or sky-blue, it wouldn't be so horrifying.'

'Blood is always blood. What does its color matter, Ma'am?'

Mother ignored Felisa's reply and asked about Ramón. The old woman became disturbed and attempted to divert attention away from the question by rearranging Mother's pillows and tidying up the magazines left forgotten on the bed. She placed the cellphone on the nightstand, stretched the linen sheets that she herself had embroidered, and shook the quilt. She, Mother, had been a child happily given over to being cared for by others. Felisa thought of Matías and the pigs to erase the image of Ramón, and before Mother asked about him again, she said – with a cruelty that surprised even herself – that the Little Girl was no longer a baby at the breast and it was impossible that she could have heard her crying all day.

'She must be about twenty-five now, Ma'am. I don't think she'll stay here very long. She'll leave as soon as she can.'

'I don't like hearing her cry.'

Felisa didn't answer. She glanced at her wristwatch and saw that the long hand was about to hit the fifty-ninth minute. In no time at all, it would be seven o'clock.

'I'm sure they've gone to fetch Mister Cándido. Your daughter, Ma'am, no longer has anything to do with this world, and nails are going to start growing out of her head,' Felisa protested. She imagined the Little Girl vomiting the entire contents of the hardware store. She remembered her as a baby trying to bite off people's big toes and sucking anything she came across while crawling on the floor: toes, nails, corners, knees, pointy shoes, heels...

'Would you mind if I had a cigarette?'

'Now?' Felisa was struggling to tuck the corner of a sheet that was fighting to free itself from its fate under the mattress.

'Yes, right now,' Mother said. 'I feel so hot...'

Miss Felisa opened the window and left the room. She returned shortly after with an ashtray and the box in which the tobacco and the lighter were kept. She placed the ashtray on the night table. Mother reached for a cigarette and Felisa brought the flickering flame closer. She inhaled gently and, with the same smoothness, placed herself under the rays of the sun falling on the pillows. She looked at the ceiling. She smoked, and expelled the smoke so sparingly that she appeared to be breathing in the midst of some pleasant dream. Felisa sat at the head of the bed, monitoring each of Mother's movements with the lit cigarette. Mother, who continued to look like a portrait of a deceased girl, stretched out her hand and tried to touch the box. She caressed it without looking at it, sighing at the delightful pleasure of tobacco, muttering something Felisa couldn't understand. She didn't want to understand, and that kept her from asking. But Mother turned toward her, and as she expelled a cloud of smoke, dared to ask:

'How long has it been since Ramón died?'

It was an odd question and Felisa didn't know whether to remain quiet or tell the truth. She coughed, looked at the TV set, closed her eyes and coughed again. She brought the wooden box closer for Mother to caress, but above all else to distract her and not to have to answer. Mother took the box. It was a rather large box, hard to hold with a single hand. But it was a silent box. It had been born to conceal secrets. On its lid, a kimono-clad woman held a basket of cherries under a flowering cherry tree.

The red color of the cherries made her think of blood, and as if taking a suicidal leap into an abyss, the image of the scorched pigs made her shut her eyes tight. Felisa felt the urge to cry.

We spent the afternoon visiting stores. The old hardware store still had the sad gray color that clung to the walls after the fire and could not be removed, no matter how much paint was applied. The employees, dressed in the same navy blue smocks I'd remembered since childhood, greeted me with a distant respect. I didn't feel at all happy there. I was uncomfortable, tired, and things kept sliding past me without stopping anywhere. I even thought they would disappear if I touched them. They had the inconsistency of overexposed photos. I received a message from Angela in the mid-afternoon. The cellphone vibrated in my handbag and I didn't want to read it, I don't really know why. 'What time must it be in San Diego?' I wondered. It must be dawn. I remembered I hadn't even told her I'd arrived safely, and had the feeling that she had definitely vanished from my life. We visited the city's three stores. 'Our stores,' as Aunt Natalia liked to say. She ruminated over those words and pronounced them with infinite pleasure.

Our, softly and with delight, as though drinking mint-flavored chocolate.

Stores, with reverence, as though speaking of a powerful deity.

I always thought I could hear the bright tinkling of money behind Aunt Natalia's cheerful voice. She was enthusiastic about the sales assistants' new uniforms: blue dresses with the discreet store logo embroidered on the lapel. They looked like tall, slim, solicitous flight attendants. They were delighted to learn who I was, took an interest in Mother's illness (although some didn't even know her), and showed me some of the nicest items in the shop, which were the same nicest items in all three shops in the city.

'We have fifty like this one distributed in about forty cities. I don't know exactly how many. It was your mother who kept track of the accounts. I've never had a head for numbers.'

At teatime, she gave me a surprise. She told me that the family had decided to make me the sole heir to the small empire of bolts and methacrylate jars. Bearing in mind the fact that my uncle and aunt had never had children and I was the family's only direct descendant, she believed it was my right. It was a responsibility I most certainly didn't want to undertake, but when the time came we'd see how the situation panned out. I knew I was planning a future of my own choosing at the expense of the hardware store and houseware establishments, and I also knew that once it was in my hands, once I was in a position to take on the annual migration of whales, the family's commercial interests wouldn't matter to me at all. I immediately replied to Natalia's proposal with a smile and a 'yes.' The problem arose when she lit a cigarette and assumed that serious, dressed-up voice she reserved for delicate situations.

'The trouble is, Child, that your mother is in no state to do anything. And it looks as if she never will be. She has her good days, true, but otherwise all she has is a hole in the head. Your uncle's no good for this work. He's good at dealing with our regular customers at the hardware store all day.' She took a few drags from the cigarette and a sip of coffee, adding, 'And as for me, I'm no good at these things, Child.' The waiter had left a bowl of cherries steeped in moonshine on the table. Aunt Natalia ate them one after another, leaving the pits in a pile on the saucer of the coffee cup. 'So we have a problem. A lovely, big, fucked-up problem.'

Those words – 'lovely, big, fucked-up problem' – reminded me of something, but I didn't know what. It was like a lullaby I'd been sung a thousand times in childhood, which excited me if I heard it from the lips of a stranger in a place that wasn't their own. The lullaby came back and, coupled to it like the cars of a train, brought back the memory I'd believed to be completely lost.

'What's the problem?' I was very tired, I had just travelled thousands of kilometers, and it didn't seem to matter to anyone. To them it was as if I'd merely gone out one Sunday afternoon to buy an ice-cream cone and returned in less than an hour with my mouth stained with chocolate. She hesitated. Aunt Natalia had a nervous tic that only manifested itself during extremely awkward moments: her forehead would wrinkle and straighten out again. She probably didn't realize it, but its effect on those present was particularly comical. At that moment she furrowed and unfurrowed her brow.

'We think that you should be in charge of managing the companies. You'd have to come over here, of course. You'd have to quit your studies.'

I was disconcerted by this, and disappointed. An uncomfortable, hot sensation crept up my legs to my thighs, and my abdomen trembled with anguish. The worst was yet to come:

'And mind you, this isn't me saying it, but your mother and your uncle. But if you don't accept, it's likely you'll be cut out of the inheritance.'

I started pecking at the cherries, like she did. I didn't know what to say. I felt trapped, betrayed. Exhausted. I told her that what she was proposing was unjust. As she watched the smoke rising from the cigarette on the ashtray, Natalia answered in a tragic, all-knowing tone:

'There is no justice, little one. What do you find unjust? Do you find it unfair that we've supported you all these years? Do you find the three thousand euros you receive each month unfair?'

It wasn't easy seeing Aunt Natalia angry, but at that point she'd raised her voice more than was normal. When she did this, that happy, musical, and sometimes grave voice would turn into a ludicrous cackle that would immediately shatter her eternal elegance, no matter how tall, slim, and deafening she might be. Suddenly conscious that the shouting marred her immaculate presence, she grew quiet and didn't speak again until I asked why, if she wanted me to stay in the city, it had pleased her so much to have me learn how to scuba-dive.

'Because I don't even know how to swim.' She didn't look at me. She picked up her bag from the back of the chair and began walking toward the exit.

We walked together, but without speaking. Neither one wanted to take the other by the hand to convey a sense of calm. Natalia didn't even try to justify what I'd said. Silence. We walked in a sad silence and the fact is that I was greatly hurt by the wrath and deception that were conveyed to the flagstones by her heels, forced as they were to follow a rushed, angry pace to which they were unaccustomed. She accompanied me home and entered Mother's room for a moment, shutting the door behind her. I sat down in the living room, like a punished child. Felisa appeared suddenly, and since she knew something, asked me if I was pleased with the gift.

'They always give me something I don't want.'

'You've been here one day and you're already thinking about leaving.' She seemed annoyed.

'I'm only visiting,' I answered, vexed. Intimidated, she left.

'I don't know what it is you're missing away from home!' she shouted as she walked down the hallway. I felt like chasing after her and giving her a few slaps.

The box was delicate, silent, unobtrusive. It had been built to be discreet, in spite of the gaudy drawings that adorned it. Discretion has nothing to do with showiness of form or excess of color, but with the place the object will occupy in someone's life. The place assigned to the box – and therefore there'd been no arguing over its decoration – was the intimacy of shadows. Shadows would take care to blend the bright tones of the red, blue, and green colors and the aggressiveness of the black looks and the yearning for flight of the birds decorating the kimono of the woman sitting under the cherry tree. Shadows would know how to give her white, feminine cheekbones a soft, pinkish hue, and give her a smile and a welcoming embrace when she was viewed, in private, in an intimate location.

The box made no sound when opened, and didn't even sigh if it was. If someone closed it, it would be with such care that the lid never struck the body. If that did occur, if it was struck, because human beings had displayed their emotions, the box was prepared for silence: its wooden edges were decorated with silk and the box would keep silent, no matter how much someone tried to make it resonate. It would swallow its own secrets. It wasn't alive, but neither was it dead. It didn't hear, but neither did it have any intention of speaking.

Father had brought it, the man I could only evoke through Mother's rusted hatred, and whom I could intuit from afar whenever I saw a ship. He brought it from overseas in a suitcase, kept in his captain's quarters. Mother had liked it, although when Father placed it in her hands, she knew it wasn't entirely her own, that other hands had caressed it before hers and that it held a secret that Father would never bring himself to reveal to her. Whenever she came close to the box, she noticed a delicate scent like gently perfumed water. A smell that was distant and kind. It settled into her hands like a tender, homeless kitten that she took in without question. However, although she gave in to Father's embrace once again, she knew that the silent box, made for the shadows, had been given to her with the devotion and cowardice of a parting gift. She accepted them both: Father in her bed and the box in her life. In the few weeks that Father was home, she even had the courage to ask him for another child.

'I need a Little Girl. Someone will have to look after Ramón when I'm gone.'

She asked this of him as if agreeing to the purchase of a car, or a freezer in which half a side of beef could be preserved. And from there, from that explicit and satisfied desire, I was born.

I was looking at the box, trying to describe it for inclusion in the *Anthology of Quotidian Objects* in my own handwriting, when Aunt Natalia emerged from her room and sat beside me. She was trying to be nice, trying to apologize. She was trying to get me to understand her disappointment because I was the only young person on whom they could rely.

'You know? What hurts me the most is that it was you who encouraged me to leave, and now you want to tie me down to something in which I'm not the least bit interested.'

'But we're the ones who support you, and life isn't always about doing what we want, my dear child.'

Once more I was overcome by the tiredness that had gripped me during the afternoon. I remembered that two days previously I'd been stretched out on the beach drinking tequila with Kazuo and Angela. I remembered that in the room at the end of the hallway was my mother, the centrifuge victim, utterly spent. I took a deep breath, took my aunt's hand, and told her we would speak at a later time. She left. I started walking silently and slowly toward Mother's room. I heard Felisa in the kitchen singing a bolero and the sound of a pan boiling on the fire. As I walked, I thought Ramón would continue to be my destiny.

It was all the same to me that Ramón had been dead for fifteen years.

Felisa left the attic where Mother had placed her when she came to look after me, and moved into the room that had been Ramón's. I wondered if the wisterias that when in bloom would invade the staircase with a violet aroma would still be clinging to the vine on the terrace. And what of the planters filled with the fleshy, euphoric hydrangeas that would press against each other in an effusion of wine-colored petals when they blossomed? Would the petunias that dangled from the stone balusters still be there, invading the summer sky with the curious, colorful funnels of their corollas?

Felisa was so proud of her urban garden – that paradise on high that was only hers, and mine – that she would show it off with theatrical generosity to the old clients of the arts-and-crafts shop for which she had worked as an embroiderer and who still assigned her projects. Some of them would have died to have embroidered sheets in stitched mesh. Others wanted tablecloths in nautical mesh, and the more modest ones hankered after fine, diminutive handkerchiefs festooned with double hemstitch outlines. The most difficult, the most expensive, the most arduous and the least satisfying – because it was never as perfect as she would have liked – was the Richelieu embroidery. No matter how much money she was offered, she only accepted it on rare occasions. She'd make an unhurried appraisal of the items that still remained to be embroidered, and if there were too many of them she used me as an excuse to reject the assignment.

'I can't concentrate on such delicate work with the Child underfoot. You've got to invest all your five senses into this kind of work, on such fine cloth.'

She never accepted embroidery in colored thread, either. Or silver or gold. Despite her fondness for the gaudy – you could tell from the prints on the clothing she wore, from the paint she used as make-up, from the little glass figures crowding the furniture, the shelves and any other flat surface in the house unable to rebel against such a ghastly, strident mix of forms and colors – she could only embroider in white thread.

'Multi-colored embroidery is really tawdry,' she would say, and end up convincing her clients that hunting scenes against autumn backgrounds, embroidering oak trees in yellow and brown, and the blood of hunted animals shot through by arrows in browns and reds were in very poor taste. She also convinced those clients, who were only looking for a wedding present at an accessible price, that a cross-stitch tablecloth with green and reddish geometric figures was an absolute vulgarity, especially if they tried to reproduce baskets of cherries or roses in those colors. Elegance – art – lay in knowing how to embroider in white. White embroidery, well done, is fit for a king's table.

Later, very theatrically, dressed in an unforgettable profusion of orange hibiscus against a pink background, she'd show off the tranquility of her urban garden to her clients. When I was still a baby, I would take advantage of the presence of so many knees and suck on them. Some clients put up with my loathsome indecency because they were shy. Others would dig their nails into my head until they managed to free themselves from my delicious obsession. More than one had their stockings ruined and their legs drooled on.

Well, Felisa left her attic. I found out the second day I spent at home. On the first day I was so intent on not feeling anything that I assumed Felisa would go up to her endearing little apartment after dinner, as she had done all her life. It was the next day, before Aunt Natalia turned up, tall, slender, and elegant, when my steps led me to

Ramón's room. I expected to find the old Kent Miller marine action figure, missing a leg and scattered on the rug. I was expecting to find the blossoming geranium near the window, and touch it to feel – as I had done for years – the beating of a heart that weighed at least four hundred kilos. I was expecting to open the dresser and recognize the manic arrangement of the clothes it contained: T-shirts and underpants folded in the top drawer, socks in the middle drawer, and pajamas in the third, at floor level. I was expecting to be caressed by the smell of my brother's bath cologne. But when I opened the door, I found Felisa sitting up in bed, wearing a terrycloth nightshirt stamped with small flowers, trying to put on some nylon stockings. I excused myself and slammed the door shut. I nearly lost my appetite for breakfast. I didn't like the fact that Felisa had violated the intimacy of a space that was sacred to me – and to Mother as well, or so I thought. Even so, it gave me enough time to make out the intensely red geraniums flowering on the desk at which Ramón would sit at night, solemnly reading his comic books and Jules Verne adventure novels. I had enough time, however, to realize that one of the first things I had done was rescue the old Kent Miller marine action figure from the bottom of my backpack and place it on my nightstand. Kent Miller was safe. And I suppose the dresser contained – rather than Ramón's clothing – Felisa's neatly ironed, folded, quiet underwear.

What became of Ramón's underwear, T-shirts, socks and pajamas? Where they being kept somewhere in the house or did they wind up in a Salvation Army clothes bin? How was it that Mother, having kept that room as a shrine, had agreed to allow Felisa – whom Ramón had hated so much – to occupy his endearing space? Seen from a practical standpoint, and holding onto my initial intent to see without feeling, there was an explanation. Mother needed continuous supervision. A shout in the middle of the night demanded a presence that only a hearing person could offer.

But I wondered if Mother knew, and I was very nearly sure that she had no idea that Ramón's sanctuary had been profaned. I'm sure she thought the house was exactly the same as it had been two years ago, when she crossed the threshold to her room and decided not to come out again.

She did agree to widen her bathroom for the sake of comfort. I know this because Aunt Natalia told me. Mother loved taking a shower whenever she got home from touring the city in search of a new place in which to sell the tin masks, conical vases, and silverware designed exclusively for two-person families looking forward to being able to have two guests (at most) over for dinner. And she enjoyed getting into warm water before dinner, a bath in which she would linger, caressing her body with the excuse of impregnating her skin with the delightful substances she added to the water.

Ramón had also liked long baths. Especially on Sunday nights, when, submerged until he wrinkled, ten whales were born from each of his fingers.

Just as I was sure that Mother was unaware that Felisa had moved into Ramón's room, I was equally certain that she didn't know that last year, around Christmas, Father had sent a card. A stupid Christmas card with a deer and Santa Claus surrounded by glitter. On the back were five clumsily-written words that verged on the offensive: 'Thinking of you. Happy holidays.' That was all. After a silence of nearly ten years, after Mother had written him hundreds of letters crammed with rebukes and consumed by an old and corrosive hatred, even claiming his compassion, he had dared to send a sorry Christmas card with a 'Thinking of you. Happy holidays' written in a hand so tall and thin and insecure that it looked like a drawing, as if the person who had written it ignored the fact that those were words and had a meaning.

No one had told me about that card. Not even Aunt Natalia, who had told me in her undressed voice that Father had sent a letter a year ago from Osaka. Japan. She thought she'd show it to me one afternoon after we'd had some iced tea in the kitchen. She was particularly kind, trying to conceal the disgust she was still feeling at my refusal to sign away my future. She knew that the money that opened her accounts in the most exclusive boutiques in the city and in restaurants where we needed no reservations depended on my decision and my goodwill. We drank the tea, and subtly, as was her custom, Felisa left a bottle of cava on the table and some skewered meats that had only just arrived from the Japanese restaurant that had very recently opened for business on the ground floor of our property. Aunt Natalia talked about her, talked about me. She brought Mother's incurable madness to the table and even evoked the dolphin *Flipper*, which she would watch with Ramón when he was little, as a metaphor for freedom. Aunt Natalia, a little hammered by now, spoke of things I already knew and things I knew nothing about. She wept when she recalled each and every one of her abortions. She grew strong when speaking of how she confronted the breast cancer that nearly killed her and even spoke of her passion for tomatoes.

But again, the tomatoes are another story.

Meanwhile, I walked around the kitchen looking for something to distance me from her words. I felt suddenly hot and opened the window; suddenly cold and I'd close it. I noticed how she dug a nail from her left hand into the middle finger of her right hand. She talked and talked. I went out to the hallway looking for Felisa, but she was praying the rosary, kneeling on the carpet on which Ramón would place his bare feet when he got out of bed in the morning. Every time I went back to the kitchen, Aunt Natalia's lipstick had run a little bit more. A little bit more. Her words sprang from the atrocity of not having anyone to talk to. It was a fireworks display. At last she stopped talking.

I finally sat down beside her and smoked a cigarette. I thought this was the required silence before we dispersed, like when we were children and played in the park until the savings-bank clock struck seven or eight and each of us walked home, like robots. But Natalia still had one surprise left. She left the kitchen and came back with an envelope. There was a card inside the envelope. On the back of the card someone had written, 'Thinking of you. Best wishes.'

'That isn't Father's handwriting,' I said.

'No, I don't think it is, either.' She wasn't wearing any lipstick, and her words seemed more credible to me than when her lips were smeared in pale pink. 'It looks more like a child's handwriting.'

'Does Mother know?'

'Why should she? The less she knows the better. Don't you think?'

Possibly. That question seemed sufficiently tortuous and interesting to entertain me for hours.

'I am your gift. Unwrap me.' These words were written on a somewhat faded apple-green card, kept in a dresser drawer inside a silk-wrapped box that contained a delicate, transparent set of lace paper. A set of baby-doll pajamas. The handwriting on the card was Mother's. I'd read it many times when I was a girl, during my clandestine visits (she would have called them sinful) to a woman's intimate belongings. My mother's. I didn't understand what the words meant until one afternoon, on the way back from school, Mother phoned me to say that she was in the hospital with Aunt Natalia. Natalia, at her age and unexpectedly, had become pregnant and spent half her life hospitalized. Despite all the care, she'd had a miscarriage when she was five months along. It was very sad.

'Start studying,' she commanded. 'I've already told Felisa to make you supper.'

I hung up the phone and rushed to my parents' room. I did what any girl my age would have done. I must have been twelve years old at the time. I tried on clothes, shoes. I put on make-up, applied perfume, admired myself in the mirror and wondered what I would look like at twenty. I caressed Father's clothes, sniffed them for quite a while, hoping to find the remnants of a scent I'd never been able to enjoy. That afternoon, knowing I had all the time in the world, I dared to remove the two items that were as delicate as sea foam. Yes, there was something foamy about them, reminiscent of salty liquid. I undressed slowly in front of the mirror, and I think I enjoyed the sight of my naked body for the first time, with my breasts starting to appear like small flour volcanoes and my waist insisting on curving inward. What fascinated me most was admiring my soft, brown, scarce pubic hair. I had seen Mother naked many times when I was small. I'd seen her hike up her skirt and drop her underpants to pee and I was fascinated by the shock of red hair that lit up her thighs. I now remember how uneasy I'd felt at the sight, as if there were something sinister lurking beneath that mass of hair. My own newly-grown hair, almost like the soft down that covered my legs, was not as dense as hers. It curled and had an aggressive brown color that wounded my white skin. I thought it looked like Father's beard – brown, short, but curly. Though lighter.

I then got dressed, slowly, with the baby-doll set hidden in the box like an unspoken desire. They consisted of two pieces: a little pair of French panties and a sort of T-shirt in green hues, trimmed with green and white lace. Green sea foam. They were soft, like soapy water slipping through one's hands, like Ramón's chest when he emerged from spending hours in a relaxing bath and held me in his arms because I was still a baby. I put on the French knickers. They were too big. I held them from the back with one hand, tightening them against my abdomen. They rubbed against my thighs, causing an electric shock – that first, odd, tingling sensation. I was no stranger to it, having felt it perhaps in some dream or in the shower, as hot water slid down my abdomen and vanished between my thighs. I was scared, but kept clutching the pants against my mound of pubic hair and put on the chemise with my other hand. It was large, but it didn't matter because I felt very beautiful.

I lay down on the bed and spent a long time looking at myself in the mirror. The apple-green card was telling me, 'Unwrap me.'

'I'm your gift. Unwrap me.'

I began freeing myself from those clothes as if they really were gift wrapping. I remained on the bed, lying down in front of the mirror. And I finally understood. I imagined Mother lying down, dressed in that moist, soft way and with the apple-green card between her breasts. Meanwhile, Father looked. Father kissed, Father licked, Father desired her so much his genitals burned. Then Father would unwrap her.

And I know what they were feeling because I felt it too. I knew, without anyone explaining it to me, how to satiate that first raw burst of desire, because at the very same moment it became insatiable I also intuited where it was coming from. Where it was coming from and how to calm it down.

I felt electric, I felt liquid.

One afternoon as we were discussing my relentless rebellion, my urge to flee from any imposition that would cut off my future, Mother remarked that I was like Father, always swept along by a silent, invisible wind that could even be noticed in photographs. In pictures of me, the few in which I appeared, I could be seen shattering the verticality of the rest of the people having their photos taken, the landscape, and even the orders given to me more than once by the photographer. I was always tilting sideways, as if pushed by a raging wind. Not even my features were as clear, as well defined as one might have expected. I was out of focus. I was a being forever out of focus, smiling sadly on the few occasions when I did smile. I smiled with the duty to trace an upward curve on my face so as not to look like a brute. I smiled, but I was somewhere else.

'You flee from everywhere, my child. You take after your father.'

And all of a sudden, one afternoon when we were discussing my relentless rebellion, Mother decided she wanted to write a letter. Like before, when she would write a letter on Sunday nights sitting at the kitchen table, equipped with cigarettes and bolstering her doubts with a couple of gin and tonics.

She was up that afternoon, sitting in the armchair, trying to read a book but not making it beyond the first page. Her extreme emaciation gave her outstretched, backward-tilting neck the tension of a bowstring. Something was going to shoot out at any moment.

And it did.

'I want to write a letter. I'll dictate it to you.'

She got up and opened one of the dresser drawers. She rummaged among her underwear, twisting in an unstable equilibrium between the fire in her head and the coldness of her feet covered in violet silk slippers. She approached the table where I'd been sitting, the table that had been done up like a white, virginal bride on the day of my arrival, and she put the notepaper on the tablecloth – the thin onion-skin paper of airmail letters. I looked at my hands when she placed the writing paper on the table. My first hands. I looked at the bed, at the mirror of the armoire that was always there, as huge as the whale that Ramón had tried to become. I looked at the dresser like a woman with an unmentionable secret. My unmentionable secret.

'Is something the matter, Girl?' She seemed so happy, so spotless, so far from desire that I was jolted, as if by looking at her I was looking at myself before that afternoon when I discovered pleasure, thanks to the words she'd written on a card. Without realizing it, Mother had shown me the path to sex and pleasure. I was on the verge of telling her to unwrap me, but then I remembered the moment would always arrive when I would resort to the same game with the only men I had slept with – a total of two – and that I was never able to sleep with them again because I could feel Father and Mother invading the bed. Desire would then vanish, replaced by a sticky loathing: the lover's body would turn into just another man. Skin, flesh, blood, eyes on fire, a sweat that stuck to my skin, hair that choked my throat. An urge to vomit.

'Are you all right?' she insisted.

I tried to hide it, but I was red to my eyebrows and felt as if my body were suspended in mid-air by sudden nausea. Hollow. My body felt hollow. I was floating.

'Are you feeling hot?' She was so pitilessly kind that she made me feel like an imbecile. 'It's my fault, I'm freezing to death. I asked Felisa to leave the heat on for me.'

It was July. The heat was unbearable. How could she be cold?

She hurried into bed. She arranged herself under the blankets, arranged the pillows in such a way that her red mane bunched up like a storm cloud. And from in amongst the red hair, tinted by a hairdresser who would come by once a month, her face appeared, all sharp angles and corners. The sight of her corners inspired tenderness in me, and she knew it. She knew nothing else. She had no reason to: I never told her about it. I merely wore her underwear on that occasion and left it just as I'd found it. Perhaps not as well folded. Perhaps the apple-green card wasn't where it should have been. Perhaps she held a similar ceremony every night. Perhaps she'd recognized a smell that wasn't hers on the clothing. Perhaps she knew the youthful smell belonged to her daughter. Perhaps she knew why I blushed and why my hands trembled… but she settled between the pillows, reached for a glass of lemonade that Felisa had left on her nightstand, and shuddered it down. She then took time to trace her lips with her tongue and find a posture that would allow her to look at me without effort. Impassively, without the slightest emotion on her face beyond a distant light attempting to rupture her retinas without success, she said nothing. Neither did I.

It didn't take me long to settle back into the family routine. With one of her placid, pink-lipstick-filled smiles – I don't know how she could trace with such precision the outline of lips that seemed not to exist – Natalia told me that it would be best not to talk business for a few weeks. A few weeks could be a suitable amount of time for her, but what made her suppose that this would be a useful amount of time for me? In fact my intention when I left the Bay was to return within fifteen days: hence the reason for packing so lightly and booking a return on July 14th. But no, Aunt Natalia only looked at time from her own standpoint, and now that I realized it, at no time had she asked me when I was planning to leave. No one asked me when I was thinking of leaving. It seemed that everyone, except Felisa, took it for granted that my stay would be indefinite. Angela's words of farewell resonated in me again and I remembered that I hadn't even bothered to read the message she had sent to my cellphone.

I reached for the phone and read the message: 'You've forgotten where you belong too soon. How was the trip?' Yes, those words sounded more distant to me, more unknown than the passivity and peace of Mother resting in bed.

I was thirteen or fourteen when I started going out with boys. He was called Virxilio, an odd name for such a young lad. He was affectionate, handsome, and had an admirable ability – which I grew to despise over time – to talk non-stop about the unlikeliest subjects. He was an expert at making speeches. If you showed him a potato, he would go back to the history of Mesoamerican civilizations. Utter any word – 'acorn,' for example – and he'd list all of the varieties of oak to be found in the country. He was like that all the time: when he had no words of his own, he resorted to the words of others. He delighted in availing himself of his vast archive of poetry by an eclectic range of authors.

He wasn't a bad kid, but when we broke up, he insisted on visiting me so often, and became so unbearable, that I started hiding from him. Felisa would take care of making my apologies. She would say I was off at my uncle and aunt's villa or that I'd gone to the movies with a girlfriend. On one of those occasions when he announced his arrival (and Matías was the one who announced visitors over the phone), I hid in Ramón's old room and heard Felisa tell him I'd gone out somewhere, she didn't know where, with some girlfriends. Felisa would go out to open the door with the work she'd trapped in her embroidery frame and the needle in her hand. He asked her what she doing. She showed him the embroidery.

'Richelieu stitch. It's very difficult work. Few people know how to do it correctly.'

A little while later Virxilio was in the living room sitting with Felisa, astounded by the delicate way she handled the tiny needle. From Ramón's room I could hear Virxilio talking on and on about Cardinal Richelieu and the Three Musketeers. I could hear Felisa going into the kitchen with the excuse of kneading pasties, and I could hear him following her, talking incessantly. I smelled the aroma of onion and white tuna frying in the skillet, and also Felisa's anguish at not being able to get rid of that voice that wouldn't quit. Virxilio's voice was a runaway well spring, without a conduit to control it. I heard Mother arrive and I heard how he flattered her. I heard Mother asking after me and I was hurt by Felisa's silence, as she had no convincing reply to give her. I heard the unfair scolding Felisa had to endure for protecting me, and finally I heard Virxilio saying goodbye from the hallway. Then I came out. I wasn't as concerned with the slap that Mother was going to give me as with a desperate urge to pee. It was humiliating, like when I was small and at school and held back the urge to pee to avoid standing up in class and asking for permission to go to the bathroom. Yes, I found it humiliating. Virxilio had also humiliated me that day without realizing it.

But this isn't the story I want to tell.

I wanted to say that that Virxilio, educated, handsome and intolerable when he spoke, did manage at first to get me to fall in love with him. He was the first person I fell in love with, without counting a classmate from my earliest school days named María Helena, whom I could not keep myself away from and dreamed of every night. I remember one day that I had a massive fever and felt as devoid of strength as a dying person must feel, thinking I would die from one hour to the next. I remember asking Mother whether, in case of my death, I might be buried with María Helena. It was the only thing that would make death bearable. At the time, I didn't have the least idea what death was. It might have been something like running over a lawn and falling flat, arms outspread, onto fresh grass. It might have been that place where white threads turn into lovely embroidery.

Whatever became of María Helena? I hadn't seen her for so many years that the scallywag might have died already and not thought to take me with her.

I wanted to say that Virxilio had made me fall in love with him. Aside from my own hands and Ramón's distant caresses, he was the first person who made me feel a special, electric pleasure when he touched me. But the same thing happened to him with caresses and kisses as with words. There was no way of stopping him. If the two of us were alone, he'd find my mouth and stick his tongue down to my entrails. He wouldn't stop kissing me. Constantly, constantly, constantly. I liked the way he kissed. Besides, he had been the first one to kiss me by parting my lips and seeking out my tongue. No one had ever kissed me like that. María Helena had kissed me on the lips once, to see what it was like, and promptly spat, as if revolted. I also spat, although I'd felt no revulsion. I hadn't felt anything at all. Neither good nor bad. I had spat forward, trying to make my saliva reach further than María Helena's green and repentant gob of spit.

I wanted to say that Virxilio sickened me with so much kissing. He insisted on squeezing my body in search of breasts that didn't exist yet, no matter how much I dreamed of them as rounded, sharp and stiff like those of Aunt Natalia. One day I refused to kiss him and he asked me why. I replied that I was fed up. Fed up? Yes, I'm fed up with so much kissing every minute. How can you be fed up with kissing? I'm fed up. Why?

'I really like the tortilla that Felisa makes.'

'What does tortilla have to do with kissing?'

'A lot. I like tortilla when Felisa makes it on Sundays. If she makes it every day I get tired of it and I don't like it anymore.'

'You're mad. Barking mad.'

And Virxilio, on account of the words and the kissing all over the place, left me and found another mouth and another poetic field willing to be sowed. Although he pursued me so many times after that, and so exhaustingly, that I was forced to hide from him. Poor Felisa. I ought to think of gestures of that sort when he approaches me again, brimming with affection. Poor Virxilio.

I could use words like happiness, pleasure, pride, elation, ambition, emotion when I was far from home. But as soon as I returned, like now, I felt coerced into being happy. Those women looked at me, and if they didn't see a happy person they would level the most awful suspicions against me. They accused me of being haughty:

'But you have everything you want! You've got to stop putting on that bitch face!'

That's what it was like before I left, when they would smother me with constant kindness, and I rebelled, sometimes violently, against the permanent monitoring to which I was subjected. I was dazed by so many gifts, most of them unwanted and unasked for. And it seemed that everything was going back to normal.

'I don't know why you're making such twisted faces, Child. Aren't you happy at home?' Aunt Natalia demanded my presence day after day. Felisa was intent on making me eat the most delicious dishes she knew how to cook – at all hours of the day. Uncle Cándido would invite me to the villa with annoying insistence, saying the pool was full and I could take a dip. Mother was the only person who left me in peace, which was rather surprising, being Mother. If she was well, we could hold a conversation, and she would even dictate fragments to me – a little bit every day – of that letter she had decided to write.

But I never laughed. There was nothing new in that: I almost never laughed at home. It was always outdoors that laughter turned into an indispensable facet of my personality, and friends, even Virxilio, knew me as a happy girl. It seems that happiness is only acknowledged if you laugh at all hours, guffawing, shrieking, scattering bits of joy everywhere. Kicking up a lot of golden glitter dust. Even when it's false, people find laughter easier to bear than a stern face. They don't take into account the easy, gentle and subtle gestures with which you move. The tenderness with which you treat family, the few friends you have left in the city, almost don't count at all. You aren't fun, you aren't able to draw a permanent smile on your face. And if the situation becomes permanent, they'll bestow upon you such descriptions as embittered, resentful, sullen. Bad-tempered child.

I only knew one person who was permanently happy: Ramón. I brought this up in a conversation with Aunt Natalia.

'Ramón was ill, poor thing,' she answered maliciously. 'He was clean off his head.'

Only when I wasn't home could I freely use words such as happiness, pleasure, pride, elation, ambition, emotion – and savor their true meaning.

'It's a nice day for you all,' Felisa was bold enough to say when she scraped past my elbow with Mother's food tray. She didn't dare look up, and with a hypocrisy that verged on the obscene, I kissed her on the head. She responded as though I'd just pressed her joy button: she looked up rapturously, compliant, and with a slight tremor on her lips.

'You're too old, Felisa. You shouldn't be here looking after someone who's ill. Someone should be looking after you.' It wasn't my intention to hurt her, but she stared at me as if I'd stranded her in the desert. I tried to correct myself. 'You've been looking after others for so long. Don't you think it's time someone made dinner for you?'

'I can still take care of myself.' She got angry and rushed toward the kitchen, fearful that she would be sent off to a rest home. Perhaps she would spend some nights unable to sleep peacefully, but maybe that would convince her once and for all that I wasn't the daughter she'd yearned for so much. At least she'd stopped following me around like a love-starved dog. She kept her distance, which was exactly what I wanted. I couldn't bear another display of affection like the one that first day. There was no way I would be willing to endure the loud rebukes she aimed at me against the corridor walls. Nor could I forget the trap she set for me when I was a baby, tying me to her in bed with a rope as a reminder of a nap, while the sunbeams that came through the curtains became a noose that would bind me forever. The witch had known how to tie me to her for a lifetime. I would never be able to forget her. I would remember her every time motes of dust danced in a sunbeam in a shadowy room. The babysitting tick. The embroidering cockroach. She, the turtle unable to strip naked.

When I finally got past the barricade of Felisa's curves and managed to enter the room, I found Mother sitting at the table that faced the window and occupied the open space between the curtains. You could see the branches of the linden trees that survived in the few places where there was a break on the sidewalk.

'When they let me smoke, I try to place the butt into the hole between the branches. Can you see it?'

I saw it. It was black, round, and must surely stink of nicotine.

'Do you still smoke? Maybe you don't. I suppose you're an ecologist who doesn't smoke, drink or eat meat. When they came from the town hall to tell me that I had to separate glass from plastic and organic matter in different bags to save the planet, you know what I thought?'

I waited respectfully for her to keep talking. But she seemed to lose interest. I asked her:

'What did you think?'

'That the Earth will know how to save itself without us. Do you eat meat?'

'Yes, Mommy. I eat meat, I smoke, and I drink.'

'I'm glad to hear it.' She paused. 'Now that those witches aren't around, why don't you light up a couple of cigarettes? Let's see who can pop the butt into the hole!'

'Weren't you going to dictate me a letter? Who is it to?'

She gave me a mischievous smile, like a girl who fancies herself in possession of a secret that she's unwilling to share without a reward. I promised to fetch the cigarettes. She took the ballpoint pen and drew a stick figure on a piece of paper. She placed a cap on the figure and wrote the words 'High Captain' in a shaky hand. I was worried. For a second I thought she was going to tell me the letter was for Ramón. A warm breeze and the sound of motorcycle exhaust drifted in through the window. When she felt like it, she looked at me again, cheerfully, and said:

'Your father. Who else would it be for?' She paused to look at me. 'Do you think he's still alive?'

'I don't know, Mommy. What do you think?'

I went for the pack of cigarettes. While I lit them, Mother got up and approached the window. She didn't want to smell too much like smoke in case Felisa or Natalia should walk in and scold us.

'He's still a young man. He turned sixty-two in April.'

It was getting dark. The street lamps came on; in a building across the street a yellow light illuminated a room hitherto ignored, and it became filled with life. One child. Two children. A woman. A man. An elderly man. A TV screen glowed, and a quick repast of sandwiches and soda filled the room until someone lowered the blinds. Mother pitched the cigarette butt, aiming at the hole in the tree, but the live cigarette butt landed on a parked motorcycle. With a look, she dared me to do the same with mine, and I did it with so little enthusiasm that it remained burning for a few seconds, clinging to life in an empty flowerpot on the balcony of the apartment below.

'I'm tired,' she said, and closed the window. 'It's too cold for me.'

I helped her lie down and covered her up to her neck. She seemed like a bird clad in lovely bright plumage, exhausted on the snow. I couldn't understand how less than five minutes ago she had been a vibrant woman again, and how readily her face was enveloped by that tired pallor. I couldn't discern the moment when the change had occurred. Maybe it was the cigarettes, or simply an unexpected memory that had startled her and wounded her to death. Yes, it was like fast-acting venom. But I still had the feeling that all that sudden exhaustion was little more than an act, a way to instill a certain compassion in me and bind me to her to the end. How long could that agony last? Would it end in a few days or would she shrivel away in bed until all that remained was bones, skin, and eyes disturbed by the reddish fog of fever?

If previously, during all the time I had lived with her until I was nineteen, she had been a hostile, violent, and insulting woman, she could not suddenly hope to awaken in me something resembling affection. She was my mother, but I don't remember her ever giving me a kiss in all my life. Though she looked so fragile, I don't even remember a caress that might have moved me. Nor was it strange that I should question her illness, I was so worn out by her past trickery. But for once it was true: she wasn't faking it. I felt her breathing become slow, very slow, and called for Felisa.

Felisa was in the kitchen, gutting breams. She came running with her hands still covered in blood and remnants of fish gills. She looked at us from the doorway, went away and returned soon after, cleaned up, and bearing a soda bottle half full of a transparent liquid that she poured on her hands. She leaned over Mother and rubbed her forehead. A debilitating smell of moonshine invaded the room, filling my soul with an odorous, narcotic silence. She then rubbed Mother's arms and legs. Felisa was admirable. Unable to do anything at all, I remained standing by the bed, experiencing a moment that was completely alien to me. I recalled once again the sick child, Lurdiñas, who would be macerated in rum to bring her back to life. Felisa, the embroidering spider, was truly an expert at resurrections, because Mother, possibly drunk as a cherry, opened her eyes in no time at all and asked us to turn on the TV for her.

'If she stands up for too long, her blood pressure drops,' the expert masseuse warned me, closing the bottle and taking it with her back to the kitchen. I pictured the bream, open and gutted on the marble countertop, being revived by the alcoholic aroma of the old nanny's hands.

'We'll continue tomorrow,' said Mother, closing her eyes.

We'll continue tomorrow. We'll continue tomorrow… I had been home for a week, and at no time had she asked me when I was planning to leave. We'd begun the letter, a surprisingly tranquil, calm letter in which, without apologizing, she acknowledged having accepted Father's silence as the only possible response to all the rebukes, insults and hatred she'd sent him in envelopes from all over the world – often accompanied by our photographed bodies – to be placed in his hands and poison him by the mere touch of the envelopes. However, she appeared to be in no hurry to finish it. But time was running out for me and actually I wasn't too curious to find out how she was going to end it. How she would sign off. Whether or not she would leave open the possibility of a reunion. It was all the same to me. I even felt tempted to tell her that it was possible that Father was dead, since someone had sent a Christmas card that wasn't in his own handwriting. From Osaka. Japan.

When Felisa brought her dinner, I decided to go for a walk. I got to the park, and the darkness of the trees and sky, diluted in the yellow light of the street lamps, closed in over my head. It was eleven o'clock at night. What time was it at the Bay? What time was it in San Diego?

I reached for my cellphone and called Angela.

II

A FOUR-HUNDRED-KILO HEART

… the sound made by the day as it fills up like a glass.

Efraín Barquero

With enormous passion and intense affection he loved screws, nuts, and all those metal parts filled with small, circular burrows.

Xesús Constela

FUNNEL

Neck, head, space surrounding it and defining it. Everything can fall into its wide mouth. It's a metaphor. It's a game. It's a bundle of laughs and suddenly it's an inconsolable lament. It's the splendiferous border between the vast, unembraceable world and the delightful existence of small things. All living beings fit in the mouth of the funnel.

The funnel is the most simple engine of transformation. It's the great purifier, the necessary path to becoming what we are. We are magma, chaos, stars in conflict, ants who have lost the queen of the anthill, leaves falling in autumn from a tree that burned down in the summer. Large animals, grim volcanoes, extraordinary emotional accidents. Life exists because the funnel's neck causes it to. With and without spikes. Life in the funnel runs in through the broad mouth into which everything fits, even bewilderment and fear, even the dialectic of the dominating and the dominated, even a woman who insists on existing, regardless of what life throws at her... In its long, narrow neck, like an expressway where unprecedented things occur, leaving even the most extreme militancy bereft of arguments, life gets mixed up, genders are confused, the tortured become torturers, an opera singer spits out nails and tacks during a peaceful melody, a fat kid shelters the four-hundred-kilogram heart of a gray whale in his chest.

I see the drawing of a funnel cut out against the rest of the world. The funnel exists because everything else defines it, profiles it, refines it. Refines its shape as it refines the honed shape of a cypress tree, of a castle surmounted by a particularly angular dome. Or as it refines basins, abysses and valleys. Funnels eat, digest, and transform shapes. Perhaps they maintain their essence. They absorb the air and turn it into a dance. They absorb what emerges from the ground and transform it into light, into a challenge to the planet's convexity. The funnel is assimilated life. The channel in which the fountainhead is dominated, ordered.

The funnel is the intention of order.

It was three o'clock in the afternoon one day in early July 1987. A day in the middle of the week. They had just finished eating and Ramón burped. He opened his huge mouth so that the food he had just ingested could issue its long daily scream. He even squeezed his stomach to make sure that not a single bubble of air was left inside him. Then he stared at the tablecloth like an idiot, numb. He closed his eyes and remained still while Mother looked on, concerned and alert, for any sudden movement by her son. Mother feared that Ramón would tilt his head too far sideways and would fall to the floor, asleep. But he never fell. He didn't even move. Only every so often would his neck tilt abruptly forward and his chin hit his chest. Later, a thread of saliva would slide between his lips and hang in the air, threatening his clean shirt. It was because of that drop of saliva that Ramón still wore a bib, even at the age of sixteen. It was because of that drop, hanging like the floater on a fishing line, making one think about the stupidity of the human race.

While he nodded off, Mother cleared the table, making sure to avoid even the slightest brush against his body.

Until he woke up, removed his bib, and hoisted his hips to get up and prepare to go to work, there would be a semicircle covered in crumbs on the tablecloth from his meal. His movements when he woke up were precise and punctual. He stood up, leaving his chair slightly separated from the table, with each leg in the center of a tile. He went to the bathroom, brushed his teeth, washed his face, washed his hands. He rinsed his teeth, dried his face, dried his hands. He combed his hair slowly, lovingly, taking time to examine himself in the mirror. With exasperating precision he left each object in the place only he knew it occupied. The brush went inside the glass used for rinsing out his mouth, the toothpaste into a drawer; the towel was hung on a rack, straightened and situated in such a way that the front and back edges were at the same height. He didn't come out until he'd closed the last button on his shirt. He then smiled with satisfaction.

He had a lot of things to do before leaving the building and he did them in a manic order set many years previously. If he lost track of it, he'd become confused. Sometimes it happened with the Little Girl. Once she threw a glass of water at him while he was having one of his brief naps at the table, and he slapped her. It's true that he later apologized, explaining very calmly that he didn't like being woken when he slept.

It might sometimes happen that Mother didn't want to deal with the girl in the evenings, which happened almost on a daily basis. He'd then take it upon himself to pick her up and take her up to the apartment occupied by the nanny in the attic. He didn't like leaving her with that woman at all and, disgruntled, he'd then go off to work. If Mother stayed home, he had no idea what to do with that brief span of time that he customarily invested in going up to the apartment. It was only a matter of minutes, but they were a surplus, and he would desperately roam around the kitchen, asking 'What time is it? What time is it?' Mother was so used to this that she hardly heard him, and waited for the clock hands to mark ten minutes to four to be hugged by her son and then accompany him to the door. She could hear him jumping down the staircase, joyfully, unthinkingly, making a thunderous noise. Ramón was huge. He was a small, delicate giant.

Behind the display windows that opened the hardware store to the cool trees of the park, the birds had left a trail of black light in their wake and the clouds extended across the sky like silent, dirty bed sheets. The school bus stopped at the pedestrian crossing, as it did every day, and the children burst out running. These were the rich kids of the neighborhood who attended a private school on the outskirts of the city. Ramón enjoyed the whirlwind of voices and movements that swirled about the street when the children got off the bus and ran to meet their mothers. It was nearly seven o'clock in the evening, the time when Cándido closed the store for business and Ramón would hurriedly arrive in time to see the children fluttering around the little square that opened up to the park. They sometimes seemed like fish to him; at other times they would remind him of worms twisting inside a can of rotting flour. When among the children, Ramón was an enormous creature, a gray whale, a clumsy bear, looked upon with distrust by the adults and warmly greeted by the kids.

Ramón had never boarded a bus alone, not even when he went to school. Mother was afraid of leaving him alone, not because anyone would harm him, but because she was not entirely sure that he was as peaceful a creature as he appeared to be. He was like one of those huge, lazy dogs that spent the day sleeping in the garden, and, every so often gobbled down a cat out of sheer instinct before returning to their infinite peace and quiet, unaware that household dogs living in an elegant garden do not eat their neighbors' cats.

Ramón would leave the hardware store at seven. The hardware store was across from the park, on the corner of street where he lived with Mother and the Child. At ten minutes to seven he began undoing the buttons of the dark blue tunic that all the employees wore. It didn't matter whether there were customers or not. He was a disciplined worker, a good worker, but he knew full well that his shift was over at seven o'clock sharp. Mister Elpidio, a sales assistant who had for years been selling nuts, bolts, bits and drills, tacks and nails, was in charge of dealing with the customers that Ramón would leave stranded at the counter. With his tunic perfectly folded over his arm, he looked at the big clock that crowned the entrance of the doorway, waiting for the long hand to rise to the fifty-ninth minute before he went into the back of the shop, where he would hang up his tunic, collect his jacket, and comb his hair in front of the broken mirror hanging over a washbasin. He would clock out at seven on the dot, say goodbye with a respectful 'Good night, see you tomorrow,' and run to the bus stop.

He liked the smell of children, the mist of children's cologne, their perspiration, fresh as the sap of young trees, and that warm, happy sensation of all those hands brushing over him. He even liked the joking way – though it was sometimes hurtful – in which the kids shouted 'Ramón, fathead!' He laughed like the unselfconsciously happy man that he was, and allowed himself to be trampled by that whirlwind until the last child had disappeared, ignoring him, clutching its mother's skirt. He liked watching them disappear, carrying their backpacks, dressed in white shirts, gray suits and ties, and hard-soled shoes. He liked seeing them walk with short brisk steps, bird steps, holding onto the hands of mothers who always seemed in a hurry to get somewhere. They would go off, ending another of the magical moments that the day gifted to Ramón, and he would say goodbye to that moment with a smile, without nostalgia, and without the slightest hint of sadness, knowing they would be there again the next day.

They had been there punctually for years, at seven in the evening. Then, with a joyful smile, he would cover the scant one hundred meters separating him from the building where he lived, greeting the people he met with a correct 'Good night, see you tomorrow.' Few people answered him, but that didn't bother him. He even greeted the dogs, the trash containers, and the traffic signals. He would touch the doors of buildings with his fingertips with the intention of protecting all of the people sleeping inside them that night. He looked into businesses to say goodnight to storekeepers and customers alike, and if he saw a policeman approaching he would wait to greet him with a military salute, remind him that it was time to turn in and surrender to the changing of the guard.

This would happen in the evening. In the morning, however, when he went to the hardware store, he was always rather aggressive, and didn't have the gentle disposition for greetings and kind wishes. In the morning, when he crossed someone's path in the scant hundred meters he covered, he would only ask them the time. He could come across a hundred people and would ask the same question of all of them: 'What time is it?' Some would kindly tell him the time and he would repeat it, shouting out at the top of his voice the time he'd been told it was. Some ignored him. Some lied to him. Then there was the uncouth Señora Lucita, the butcher, who would either ignore him or tell him to go to hell, according to how things were going for her, and without even deigning to look at him.

'Fuck off, Ramón.'

'Fuck off, fuck off, fuck off…' Ramón would repeat like an idiotically blissful man who suddenly becomes unconsciously anxious. 'What time is it?'

'Five to nine,' said a kind girl walking by, dragging a heavy suitcase.

'Five to nine! Five to nine!' yelled Ramón in that waterlogged voice that tints the voices of whales dark green, nearly black. 'What time is it?'

Only upon reaching the door of the hardware store did he forget the time and wait. He looked at his wristwatch and didn't push the door inward until the large hand reached the fifty-ninth minute. He would then enter, clock in, head to the back of the store to remove his jacket and put on the navy blue tunic that he had hung next to the mirror the previous day.

On the day Ramón hit the Child, he returned from work with a present. The present was a corkscrew. The Little Girl didn't need a corkscrew at all, but it must have been the only thing he was able to spirit out of the hardware store. Ramón never stole anything. He only took things on the quiet. He would sometimes take small bulbs or clothes pins for Mother. Once he brought her a small box of multicolored tacks which Ramón and the Little Girl used to impale potatoes and carrots. They made a handful of tuber-headed dolls with those few green, blue, red and yellow tacks. Mother was beside herself with rage, ripping out the tacks, belittling her children's happy, imaginative pursuit, and returning the potatoes and carrots to their inanimate vegetable state. She hid them in some secret draw to which only she had access, and took them out every so often to pin things to the kitchen door. She used one to pin up a calendar in which a cat played with a dog. She used another to pin up Ramón's prescriptions, so as not to forget to purchase them. With a blue one, she punctured a piece of paper on which she'd drawn a heart and a tray of cupcakes traversed by a big red cross. One day she took out a yellow tack from a drawer to pin up a postcard showing a sandy white beach, seemingly surrounded by peaceful palm trees and covered by a sky that opened to infinity, reflecting the same shade of blue as the sea.

'Where did Daddy went?' asked the Little Girl, who had been talking for months now and whose mouth was filled with the desire to speak every word she learned.

'Daddy's far away, working,' Mother replied, not overly concerned whether her daughter learned words or forgot them.

'What did Daddy done in the beach?' the Child asked again, pointing at the postcard with the palm trees.

'He's not at the beach. He's on a ship,' answered Mother without the slightest shred of conviction.

She unpinned the postcard and showed it to the Little Girl. There was writing on the back, but the Child couldn't read yet. She wrinkled up her eyes like Ramón did when reading the newspaper. She put on a face as if she were in fact reading, but couldn't grasp a thing, so she continued looking at the postcard, and simply licked the water off it and then bit its corners. The Little Girl had a fixation for biting corners, even the corners of walls. She also bit shirt and coat collars, because they too were corners. At some point she nibbled at Mother's corners and even felt like getting her teeth into her elbows and knees, but Mother wouldn't allow it. She'd hit her if she tried.

She struck her in the mouth when she tried to recover her husband's postcard and found it licked and bitten.

'You have a lovely problem, Child. You have a huge, lovely problem!' And she pinned the postcard with the tack on the kitchen door again. The girl made a sad, concerned face. She looked willing to receive a huge reprimand and some whacks. But Mother headed unexpectedly for the credenza, took out a glass, and turned to the sink. She opened the faucet and let the water flow over the glass. The girl saw how Mother's body, its back toward her, began to shake, her face moving up and down with her sobbing. A while later, Mother lifted her free hand and it seemed to the Child that she was rubbing her eyes as if crying. She then went over to the table with the glass full of water and said something the Child didn't understand:

'I'd lick him and bite him too, if he were here.'

She looked at the Child with great sadness and great disenchantment, as if she had just found her dead with her teeth embedded in the corner of the building.

'We have a problem, girl. We have a huge, lovely, fucked-up problem!'

Then the front door swung open with a burst of joy that frightened the girl and Mother. Ramón looked in, and after making sure Felisa wasn't there, he entered the room with his arms in the air, imitating the grand gestures of a magician.

'Ta-dah-dah!' he exclaimed, turning right and left. As he spun to the right and to the left, Mother and the girl looked at him a little, just a little bit concerned. 'Ta-daaah! Boooooooooom, pow!'

The 'pow' was resonant, like when a bottle of cava launches its cork at the ceiling, and Ramón brimmed over with bubbles. Mother and the Child were still sitting at the table. It looked as if they were engaged in meaningful conversation. And yes, they were. Except that the Little Girl barely understood anything she was being told when Ramón interrupted them. Executing turns at the entrance to the kitchen, Ramón looked like a fat, flabby potato that gyrated and gyrated until he hit one of the walls. The Little Girl burst out laughing. Ramón made her laugh all the time, unless he was asleep. It was like having a clown all to herself, a joyful clown weighing over one hundred kilos. Ramón could eat her up if he wanted to. He could eat her up in the same way he could eat a roasted capon all by himself. He could even flatten her when he breathed. Ramón was huge. Ramón didn't fit in his room or in the entire building. Ramón only fit inside the pot of geraniums that he looked after as if his own heart were contained within. He also fit in Mother's heart and in the Little Girl's heart. But it seemed that in his father's there wasn't even space for pity.

'Ta-dah-dah!' Ramón exclaimed once more amid his shambolic pirouettes, and drew something out of his trouser pocket. Something shiny. Something the girl wasn't familiar with, but it didn't keep her from showing enthusiasm. Ramón, holding up the strange object, approached slowly, ceremoniously, and offered it to his sister.

'Corkscrew.' He said it hurriedly, and later, without looking away from the girl's shining eyes, repeated slowly, 'Cork-screw. Now say it with me: cork-screw.'

'Cwooo!' the girl repeated. Ramón broke out laughing every time the girl said 'cwoo.' And the girl laughed as well, as though drunk, infected by her brother's laughter. 'Cwooscwoo.'

Mother did not laugh. Mother had let her head fall into her hands and looked at her children, sad and disheartened, with a single eye. Ramón suddenly grew serious.

'Because I hit you, I've brought you a present.' He stroked the girl's head. She had no idea what that thing was for, resembling the outline of a tin angel. Ramón showed her. He reached for a bottle of wine, dug the pointed tip into the cork, and started threading it, watching the Little Girl with endless delight. As the curly part descended, the angel raised its wings, and the girl watched them, waiting for something incredible to happen. She was startled. When the wings touched tips on high, Ramón exclaimed as if he had just opened a gift:

'There you are! Now you have to grab one of these with each hand,' he explained, indicating the wings, 'and push them down really hard.'

Ramón was sitting on a bench with the bottle between his legs. The girl had to tiptoe to reach it. She strained with the pressure, applying sudden force to each of the wings. The bottle shot out against her body and then shattered on the floor, covering Mother's feet in wine. Mother, without raising her head from her hands, repeated her painful litany yet again:

'We have a wonderful problem. We have a big, fucked-up problem!'

The Little Girl didn't understand what Mother meant. But Ramón did. Ramón knew that the huge, fucked-up problem was him, and he was extremely hurt to hear those words. He stood up from the bench before Mother was aware of what had happened and got up from the floor herself, looking from side to side. Looking front and back, from the concave to the convex, from the largest to the smallest. Ramón saw it all, though Mother thought at times that he wasn't aware of anything. And Ramón was angry. He stared for a while, breathing, questioning, accusing, but he suddenly appeared to calm down and went over to the kitchen door. He shut it. He pointed to the paper pierced by a thumb-tack and showing a painted red heart, and looked at the two women with such love that it caused delicate waves to emerge on the postcard the father had sent. He stood there, tracing the heart's outline with his fingers.

The floor was covered in red wine, and the corkscrew's wings were hanging downwards, as if it had been the victim of some great divine tragedy. To the Little Girl, the angel appeared to be dead, lying as it was in a puddle of blood. Ramón remained standing in front of the closed kitchen door. Mother looked out of the corner of her eye at the postcard of the beach with the palm trees, and must have been waiting for the waves to be bathed in the dark tint of the wine that was staining the floor tiles. She remained silent, her head in her hands. She only perked up when the savings-bank clock struck eight outside. She then stood up, placed a pot of water on the stove, and got ready to make dinner. She only cooked when Felisa wasn't home.

The Little Girl didn't make the least effort to walk on the wet floor. She climbed onto the bench where Ramón had previously been sitting, and from that height stared at the fallen angel with outstretched wings. Ramón unpinned the postcard Mother had stuck with the tack, the postcard of the beach and the palm trees, and set it on the table. Later, and without any possible explanation, he took off his jacket and wiped the floor with it. Then, also without any possible explanation, he put on the jacket, picked up the postcard, and placed it in the boiling water that Mother had set on the stove.

'Mommy, if you look closely, you'll see the water's turning blue.'

And his mother trembled, as frightened as if she'd seen her husband's head boiling inside the pot.

Lying in bed, after imagining that beloved head boiling away in the pot, Mother thought about how hard life had been since her husband, the High Captain, had made his last journey. His absence weighed upon her, she had become sluggish and sad. It had been four years since that last trip and she remembered the farewell at the airport, knowing herself to be pregnant with the Little Girl and knowing this would be the last time she would see him, and how hard it would be to get used to his silence. Even so, she wanted him to leave. She made no effort to keep him at her side. Rather, she pushed him through the door as soon as she could so he'd disappear from her sight. As always, he seemed absent, swept by the desire to be somewhere else. They said farewell with a light kiss on the lips, an awkward embrace, and the promise of future letters and phone calls.

'Call me if there's a problem,' he said, adjusting his shoulder pads after the hug.

'I'll phone you,' she promised vaguely, wiping off with her hand the kiss that felt stuck to her lips.

She hadn't seen him since then, but would receive a phone call every two weeks, and the concierge would deliver a letter or postcard once a month, almost always on Saturday morning. Before that last trip, letters would arrive weekly and the phone would ring on Wednesdays and Saturdays. Also before that last trip, he would spend at least one month a year at home. But things weren't easy when he was home. He didn't like Ramón, and Ramón didn't like his father. He, the man, had not wanted Ramón. He couldn't understand how his own beautiful body could have produced a creature as fatuous and colossal as the few whales he'd seen in his voyages. Father didn't care about whales, or the way they sang or the way they breathed – Father liked delicate things, like the wooden box he'd given Ramón's Mommy. He liked the little colored fish that gave form to the water of aquariums. When he looked at his son, trying to show some pity, Ramón would at first look back at him with admiration, then sorrow, and, in later years, with a hatred he was unable to conceal. Ramón became so disturbed by his presence that it was necessary to summon a doctor to load him with tranquilizers, because the medications he took on a daily basis were not enough to calm him down. He became so aggressive and was so large that the High Captain was afraid of him. During that last trip, Ramón had managed to confront him and pin him between the wall and his enormous chest, and was about to strangle him with his bare hands because the Captain dared to give Mother a pot of geraniums. It was on a Sunday. While Mother made lunch, the Captain decided to buy a newspaper. He walked past a florist's displaying an assortment of small pots on the sidewalk, each with its respective geranium in bloom. That burst of color roused his good humor and even stirred up in his stomach a desire for Mother that had once been furious and insatiable, but which over time had turned into a pale demise. He chose the geranium with an almost obscene garnet tone, similar to his wife's lipstick, and bought it. He asked the clerk to wrap it in pretty cellophane and tie a golden ribbon around it. And that's how he walked into the house: the newspaper under his arm and the flowerpot held out toward Mother. And that's how he faced the sudden outburst of jealousy from his son, who emerged from the bathroom covered only in a blue-and-white-striped terry-cloth robe, and flung it against the foyer wall. The pot crashed to the floor and the cellophane issued a brief, broken sigh. Mother ran out of the kitchen.

'But the plant's for you, honey,' she thought to say, stroking the son's back to get him off his father, whom he was strangling between his hands and the wall. Between his filial jealousy and the murky guilt that sliced Mother's heart. Ramón, disarmed, pulled away from his father, picked up the stricken geranium from the floor, and went nonchalantly off to his room. He walked slowly, heavily, his flesh quivering under his bathrobe.

His father burst into tears, as did Mother. They were alone in the middle of the corridor, gasping and keeping an eye on the door that Ramón had closed as he entered the room. They hid in the kitchen. They spoke for a long time – and sometimes argued – so nervously that Mother chain-smoked several cigarettes. Every so often Mother would say:

'We have a lovely, huge, fucked-up problem.'

And Father would tell her that the best thing was to commit him to a facility. There must be places where they could look after that sort of kid.

And he said this like someone unreeling the silk from a fishing rod, wisely but with a sure hand.

Mother didn't want to send Ramón anywhere and reproached his father for not being present when she gave birth to him or afterwards. There, with the two of them shut in the kitchen, she plucked up the courage to ask him how many children he had, apart from Ramón. Reduced to a state of total moral nudity, he looked at her, lowering his gaze to the hollow of desolation that Mother cradled in her lap. He tried to lie, but couldn't.

'It's a girl. Her name's Akiko,' Father said, finally daring to face the darkness of his wife's mouth. And Mother, with a grief that deepened the black hollow of her womb, saw the man smile with pride as he said his daughter's name.

Mother rose early. She sometimes drank instant coffee and made breakfast for her children. At ten minutes to nine on the dot she would say goodbye to Ramón. She got ready and waited for Felisa to come down to look after the Little Girl and tidy up the house. She then submerged herself in the depths of the city with a fixed idea in mind, some specific destination that could be a dress she had seen days earlier in a storefront, which she recalled as being illuminated by a yearning to have it, an inspection of one of the stores she had just opened, or a visit to the hardware store to do the books, check the bills of lading, and give Cándido, her brother, some of the objects that Ramón had secretly brought home in the past few days. Cándido saw Ramón's obsession as a mere game. He, too, refrained from uttering the 'theft' word when he said Ramón had taken a screwdriver, a file, or a corkscrew. He could take anything at all because, in Cándido's eyes, Ramón wasn't stealing.

'Now if he took money, that would be another story,' he would tell Mother. 'But he doesn't seem to be very interested in money.'

Aside from doing little more in the hardware store than arranging tacks, nails, nuts, screws and any other small, precise objects kept in the hundreds of boxes that piled up on the shelves, and only dealing with customers who came specifically to purchase one of those small, precise objects, Ramón received a salary at the end of the month like the other employees. On pay day, Ramón would put his pay packet in one of his trouser pockets and, as soon as he got home, would give it to his mother, proud of being able to support that family. He would hand it to her and wait for her to make a fuss of him, like a housecat who has just caught a bird, a butterfly, or a mouse. That's how he waited, standing straight, looking forward, feeling anxious until Mother thanked him for his dedication and praised his commitment.

'If it weren't for you, my dear, what would become of us?'

Ramón had worked in the hardware store since he'd left school. He passed from grade to grade until he turned sixteen, and then a family meeting was held in which it was decided that the best thing would be to have Uncle Cándido hire him, because the kid, ever since he was little, had amused himself and calmed himself down by rummaging through the store's wares. Besides, he was kind to the customers, and the regulars had gotten the hang of his obsessive questioning:

'Do you want iron or steel tacks?'

'Steel.'

'For cement or stone?'

'Cement.'

'Large or small?'

'To hang a picture with, kid.'

Then, unable to decide, he would bring samples from each box and arrange them on the counter for the customer to choose. The job had no further complexities. It suited him well and he felt like a respectable person. He even took care to report when merchandise in the boxes was running low and it was necessary to restock. His manic obsession for having everything in its place and in sufficient quantities made him ideal for such a job. Furthermore, controlled by the effect of the medications he took at breakfast and lunch, he was a sufficiently quiet fellow not to distract the other employees.

Having him there put Mother at ease, and with time Cándido stopped having to watch him all the time. Even when Mother visited the hardware store to do the books, Ramón would greet her as if she were a vendor: he'd shake her hand and wish her 'good day.' She felt proud of that giant who'd chase her around the house demanding affection and approval, and was even jealous of a smile she might direct at anyone who wasn't part of the family. He was also jealous of unknown voices asking for her at the other end of the line when the phone rang and he happened to be the one to answer it.

They had lunch together at home every day. Sometimes Felisa was present; sometimes it was only Ramón, Mother and the Little Girl. Sometimes Cándido and Natalia were there, and when they were, Mother would make Ramón take his nap on the living-room sofa so his idiotic drool wouldn't dangle in front of his aunt and uncle. So that the moronic face he displayed when nodding off at table wouldn't hurt her so much.

When he came home from work in the afternoon when Mother wasn't home, Ramón would knock at Felisa's door, and Felisa had to drop everything to go downstairs and get the afternoon snack ready and, later on, dinner for the children. Ramón would take care of the Little Girl, whom he smothered in kisses as if he would never see her again.

'There's a gentleman with cancer,' said Ramón anxiously. The urge to tell dramatic stories of his own creation, or that twisted inside his head like the loose threads of some conversation he'd overheard in the hardware store, caused him to speak hurriedly. 'He has cancer on his face and it's eating away at one of his ears, and he's got a steak bandaged to his head. That way the cancer will eat the steak.'

'That's silly, kid!'

'I swear it's true, I saw it. The man was in the park and he showed me. His face was full of flies trying to eat the steak.'

Felisa shoved him into the middle of the kitchen, and with the Little Girl clinging to her legs like an affectionate cat, began heating water in a pot for tea. One of those delicious teas that Mother, the lady of the house, would buy at a shop downtown and serve to company – when they had any – in a delicate Chinese tea set.

'Your mother doesn't like it at all when you say such foolish things.'

'I can see,' Ramón replied, feeling his ears to make sure they were in one piece, 'that this subject is of no interest to you.'

He sat down in front of the TV and took the girl in his arms. He also inspected her ears, inside and out. He moved her hair aside with his hands and then nibbled a pink earlobe with a tiny pearl set in gold. He licked it. Felisa, who had her back to him, turned around, possessed by the permanent suspicion that they were caressing in a manner that wasn't customary between two siblings.

'But what are you doing to the girl? You don't realize you're not a kid anymore.'

The Little Girl played with Ramón's nose, put her fingers up his nostrils, and then tried to put them in his eyes. They both laughed. Felisa didn't. She took one of the cups from the tea set – because the lady of the house only liked her delicious tea served in fine porcelain – and placed a sachet containing the tea leaves inside it. She fixed her eyes on the bubbles of boiling water that she poured into the cup. Then she climbed onto a bench to reach for a box in the cupboard. It was a large, cylindrical box depicting a Little Girl of yesteryear with her hair arranged in long curls, and eating a cracker.

'I want a cracker!' exclaimed the Little Girl enthusiastically. Felisa took a couple of fat, toasted crackers out of the tin to give to each child. She placed two on each saucer, beside the hot cup. Ramón took slow, small bites out of his, knowing it was forbidden for him to eat more than one. And if he felt like having another, he would look at the drawing of the heart with a red cross and the craving would go away. He wasn't too aware of how hazardous sweets could be for him, but once he was used to the prohibition, like so many other rules imposed upon him since childhood, once he became aware of it, he accepted it as just one more of so many others. The Little Girl ate half a cracker and felt full. She threw the other half on the floor. Felisa picked it up, brushed it off with her hand, and ate it with delight.

'Are steaks good for curing cancer, or are they just to eat?'

'Just to eat.'

'How do you like them? Fried or grilled?'

'Fried.'

'Do you prefer them with rice or potatoes?'

Felisa, who was sipping the hot tea but had already eaten the crackers, knew the game and was tired of it. She knew full well how to end it.

'With lettuce.'

Ramón was startled by the reply. It was always the same: if someone didn't know the two answers he offered as the only ones possible and replied with a third option, he didn't know how to continue the conversation. He thought for a while, trying to hold onto the Little Girl in his arms as she squirmed to get to the floor.

'Well,' he said at length, 'I see this subject doesn't interest you either.'

'Thanks be to God!' Felisa exclaimed, falling silent, trying to enjoy her tea and thinking perhaps about how to best carry out an order entrusted to her that morning: table linen with twenty-four white Panama napkins. She didn't like Panama linen at all. It was a smooth fabric, too slippery for her taste, and not very delicate. If she devoted her evenings to it, that job would take a minimum of four months. She thought she'd been foolish to accept it. Lately, she got more enjoyment out of the small, pretty orders, the ones in which she could invest all her talent and leave her customers agog. She didn't need the money, either. The lady of the house had set her up in the attic apartment free of charge. It wasn't that she was paid a great deal for working as a nanny or a maid, but that she had hardly any expenses. She continued to embroider because, if she were made to stop doing what she was best at – the source of admiration from outsiders – it would be as if half her life had been taken from her.

The Little Girl walked up to a low, light green table that held colored chalk and several pieces of plasticine. The first thing she did was grab a piece of red chalk and trace a line on the floor's gray tiles. It was a poorly drawn, straight line that sometimes did its best to become a circle. When she considered the drawing complete, she proudly exclaimed:

'I maked a cookie!'

She drew another and exclaimed again, 'I maked a cookie!' and so forth until she was tired of it. Then she got up, approached the table once more, and picked up a little piece of brown plasticine. By the time Felisa had noticed her, the Little Girl had already put a vast amount of putty in her mouth. She got up with such alacrity that she dropped the delicate teacup to the ground, but managed to arrive in time to fish out a huge lump that was about to block the girl's throat. Frightened, the Little Girl started to cry and Ramón became disturbed. Like a bird startled by a sudden storm, he fluttered around the kitchen, made nervous by the shards of the teacup on the floor and by the Little Girl's crying. The Little Girl or the cup? The Little Girl or the cup? In the face of that dilemma, so atrocious for him, he was unable to make a decision.

'What's happening? What's happening?' he would ask himself, biting his hands. Felisa, accustomed to Ramón's bewilderment, had the answer: she placed the Little Girl in his arms and he did his best to comfort her. He forgot about the cup. He didn't even see Felisa bending over with a great deal of effort to pick up the shards scattered over the tiles.

'The Little Girl's hungry or the Little Girl's sleepy, the Little Girl's hungry or the Little Girl's sleepy…'

And so, that repetitive lullaby, interspersed with tear-filled outbursts that gradually calmed down as they lost strength, caused the Little Girl to fall asleep as a spot of saliva and tears expanded on Ramón's T-shirt. Little by little – and this was the magic that only Ramón was able to conjure – the stain grew larger and formed the body of a whale expelling a joyous jet of seawater at the level of his heart.

'That woman broke a cup.' Ramón was already at the door with the Little Girl asleep in his arms when his mother emerged from the elevator. All the neighbors must have heard it, because he repeated it a few more times. Ramón was like a dog: he could sense his mother from the moment she set foot in the building and would run to wait for her on the landing. And he never made a mistake: it was always her. Mother entered the house, dropped her bag and keys on the foyer table and saw that the mail consisted of only a few letters from the bank. She hung up her jacket on a coat hanger and discovered, wearily, that one of the Little Girl's stuffed animals was on the armchair. This was enough to make her angry.

'That woman made the girl cry.' Ramón pronounced *that woman* with true viciousness as he walked behind Mother like a diseased conscience.

That, with the inconsistency of his appreciation for the few people who cared for him.

Woman, with indifference and absolute disregard for the word's meaning.

As she entered the kitchen, Mother saw Felisa hurriedly cleaning away the lines that the Little Girl had drawn on the tiles. Felisa quickly asked the lady if she would like something hot to drink, but the lady said nothing. She remained stiff, her hair wild as a fit of rage, with her brown eyes scanning every corner of the kitchen. Behind her Ramón, the sharp cusp of a mountain feeding the storm, was still holding the sleeping Little Girl – accustomed to unexpected gusts of wind like a young, flexible tree – tightly in his arms.

'Haven't I told you those cups are not to be used?' Mother's eyes finally came to rest on the deep hole left by the broken cup among its fellow tea-set members. 'What do you think the everyday china's for?'

Felisa thought of the word 'mercy,' of the times she'd begged for mercy her whole life – and there had been many. She hadn't done it for a long time, at least since her husband's death, and didn't think she'd have cause to plead again, even silently, in a household as fine as this, and before such an elegant and bright lady. She resorted to one of the many stock phrases she'd memorized in earlier times, and repeated it, readying herself for punishment as she had prepared herself for insults, contempt, and the occasional beating. But the phone rang, and Mother left the kitchen in the custody of Ramón and the Little Girl – the mountain and the little tree. Felisa heard the furious vertigo caused by the missing teacup in the cabinet being unloaded on the person calling. By the time she returned to the kitchen, the nanny was getting dinner ready and Mother limited herself to saying said she could leave when the children were settled. 'Settled like beasts,' Felisa thought, and she heard, this time from the hallway, the lady's voice telling her that she would fry up a steak later on. And without another word, she headed for her room with Ramón clinging to her back.

'There's a gentleman who has cancer on his face that's eating his ear and his nose. He tied a steak to his head with a bandage.'

'Please, honey, not today.'

'It's true, Mom. He showed me. The cancer ate away his ear…'

'Please! Leave me…'

'… and the steak was full of flies.'

'… alone!'

Above the bubbling of the pot where she was boiling some slices of fresh hake, Felisa could hear the loud, sharp, fading sound of a kick against the door. Immediately afterwards she heard the girl crying and Ramón's sad lullaby in the middle of the hallway. Her stomach clenched into knot, and she knew that if only for the sake of the Little Girl, she could never leave that household.

On weekends they would sometimes go to their aunt and uncle's villa on the outskirts of the city, but otherwise they would stay home. When they stayed home, Ramón would take the opportunity to have a hot bath before Sunday dinner, a bath with chamomile salts prepared by Felisa or Mother. He spent at least an hour in the water and would emerge wrinkled and shining. He also came out very happy, with a calm smile that curved his lips toward his steam-reddened eyes.

That Sunday, Ramón spent exactly one hour macerating in the water. When he emerged from the bathroom wearing his bathrobe, the first thing he did was to look all over the house for the Little Girl to show her his pink, almost white skin, so wrinkled that it frightened her.

'If I spend any more time in the water, I'll turn into a fish. See? I already am turning into a fish!'

And right in front of her eyes he held up his fingertips, looking as if they'd been plowed by the transit of a hundred whales. Ten on each finger. Or that's what Ramón told her: that ten whales had been born on each finger. He also told her that he'd always wanted to be a whale and that someday, thanks to the baths his mother prepared for him, his dream would come true and he would go off to sea. Either flying through the air or slipping down a drain.

"What are whales?' the Little Girl asked.

'They're huge animals. The largest of them all. They live in the sea, in the oceans,' Ramón explained, going 'bop-bop' and slowly making a fish face. He kept going 'bop-bop-bop' with a balloon face until the Little Girl protested. Then he laughed and called her a silly little thing: 'The Little Girl's silly, the Little Girl's silly.' He hugged her, and settling her on his chest, stroked her hair, stroked her back. Cuddled by that huge mountain of flesh, the Little Girl had trouble breathing, but the warm, fresh smell that wafted up her nose from that body recently soaked in chamomile salts was delightful. The smell of her brother's body was more gratifying to her than that of her mother when she held her in her lap.

They played in the corridor for a while. Mother was out with Cándido, and Natalia showed up happy as the fruits she bore in her arms.

'Would you like some persimmons, Felisa? How about kiwis? There's so much fruit this year that the branches are breaking off from the weight!'

Natalia, so elegant, so slender and tall, came in burdened by a basket of fruit that, regardless of its weight, didn't throw her off balance. She pulled back from the weight, as if pregnant, and managed to stand straight on her heels with surprising aplomb. The basket must have contained at least ten kilos of fruit – more kilos than both her arms together must have weighed, even adding her breasts, even adding the skin that covered her abdomen. She wore tight pants with her hair puffed up like the protagonist of a Venezuelan soap opera. Her excessive shoulder pads made her seem as though she were dangling in the air on invisible threads. Felisa looked at her in amazement.

'Yes, Ma'am, I'll take a few.'

Natalia set the basket down on the table and Felisa, who had just hung the laundry out to dry, wiped her hands on the edges of her apron and placed the persimmons and kiwis in a pair of fruit bowls. Those left over she placed in a plastic bag to take up to her attic apartment. Felisa liked persimmons very much, but not to eat, just to leave them on the kitchen table and see them in the morning, looking radiant as she made breakfast. They gave her the will to live, they filled her with energy. They had the color of fire and the gold of sunset. She only wanted them to look at, and would take as many as she could: the greenest ones, the ones about to ripen as well as those on the verge of rotting, but which displayed an intense orange hue, verging on red. She ate the kiwis. She would slice them with a knife and take bites from them until the last green piece was left stuck to the skin.

'I make jam with the persimmons. If you like, I can show you how to make it one day when you come to the villa.' Natalia had taken a seat and watched Felisa's movements as she bit into the fruit, profiling her: the curve of her nails painted in discreet shades, always matching her clothes or, at the very least, her handbag and shoes.

Before replying, Felisa remembered that she had never been taken to the villa. Not even when the Little Girl had just been born – and if they hadn't invited her then, which was when they really might have needed her, she no longer felt she'd like to go.

'Someday, Miss Natalia. Any Saturday that suits you.' Taking advantage of the fact that Ramón and the Little Girl were somewhere in the house doing God knows what, Felisa distributed the fruit in two round bowls of chipped porcelain and then reached for some potatoes to peel.

'I wonder if you're happy here.' Natalia lit a cigarette, then searched for the ashtray everywhere in the kitchen on her own – something she'd never done before – until she found it in the dishwasher. 'Mother would never forgive me if you weren't happy.'

The paring knife fell on the table between the two women. Felisa was upset by this sudden interest on

Natalia's part, who was the daughter of a cousin she thought highly of. Perhaps she expected to be thanked yet again for having brought her to work in such a fine household, far from her lonely but pleasant existence as an embroiderer in the outskirts. Perhaps she should thank her as well for having given her the privilege of serving a half-crazed woman and a giant who appeared to entertain a constant libidinous desire toward his little sister. The only thing she could really thank her for was for having placed such a child in her hands – cheerful and lively, but with a temper as devilish as her mother's.

'It's true that Mother asks after you when I go to see her. Are you happy here?'

'Why wouldn't I be?'

She attempted to make her voice sound inexpressive but kind, as similar as she could to that of a discreet guest entering the house for the first time. Natalia amused herself by looking around the kitchen, getting up to examine a postcard pinned to the back of the door. She looked at it with curiosity, pulled it off and tried to decipher what was written on the back. The writing was blurry, washed, cooked. She couldn't read a thing and stuck it back on the door. With a gesture of contempt, she said that a postcard with palm trees could only be from that cretin.

That cretin, spoken with disgust, as if pulling the gills off a sardine.

In the hallway, Ramón had turned into a dromedary and was giving the baby a ride on his hump. The baby laughed and repeated the word 'dwo-ma-dawy,' whose meaning was completely unknown to her and which sounded empty and hollow, like an eggshell, no matter how hard she tried to pronounce the letter 'r.'

'You have a lot of patience, Felisa. You don't know how much I admire you.'

'I've learned a thing or two just by being alive. Patience is one of them.'

'I want to learn embroidery. Would you show me?'

'Yes, Ma'am.'

'In return I'll show you how to make persimmon jam.'

'Yes, Ma'am.'

'Are you really happy here?'

'If you don't mind, Ma'am, I've got to make a tortilla for the children.'

Natalia was stunned, watching her own amazement dangling from the kitchen's white light. She hadn't been expecting that reply. In fact, she had only been expecting her husband and her sister-in-law. But she didn't want to leave without having the last word. Getting up from the chair, and with the pretext of going to be with the children, who appeared to be throwing themselves against the front door, she said:

'You're not yourself today.'

Felisa waited for Natalia to go out the kitchen door before grabbing a frying pan. She even waited to pour oil into it before replying:

'Yes, Ma'am.'

Cándido wore an expression of defeat on his face as he came through the elevator door. Ramón, with the Little Girl on his back, waited for Mother to step onto the landing. As always, he had already felt her presence before Natalia and Felisa heard the muffled sound of the elevator brake. Cándido pushed Ramón away with a soft caress on his head and tweaked the Little Girl's nose before entering the house. Mother, coming behind, devoted some time to spoiling Ramón and as usual ignored the Little Girl, who sought a kiss from her that was given with no enthusiasm whatsoever.

Natalia dragged Cándido into the living room and Mother stepped into the kitchen, seasoned with the recent smell of fried onions. She entered just as the potatoes were causing the oil to bubble in the pan and Felisa was starting to beat the eggs for the children's tortilla.

'Remember not to add any salt,' Mother cautioned. Felisa felt offended and turned her back. She had been in this house ever since the girl was born, and knew the family standards well enough not to have to be reminded day after day. She, the exquisite embroiderer sought after by the whole city, was belittled by that woman like a mere servant.

Mother kissed Ramón again and allowed herself to be hugged by that fevered heart from which had sprouted two arms, two feet, and an immense head, a head too incompressible for her. When Ramón had loosened his embrace, Mother asked Felisa to open a bottle of wine and prepare a tray with ham and some cheese.

'When you can,' she ended, trying to be nice.

In the living room, Natalia seated herself on the sofa under the crammed shelves of books that Ramón had arranged by size, just like the nails and tacks at the hardware store. She crossed her right leg over her left and spilled over her husband's body like a half-melted ice cream. She was awaiting the reply to a question posed days earlier.

'It's all taken care of, little dove.' Cándido kissed her fingertips – kissed her wings to keep them still.

Mother entered the living room and sat facing the two of them. Before the wine and the skewers of cheese and ham arrived, she had already explained to those present the agreement that she and her brother had reached. She would run the company, and the profits would be split three ways: two for her and one for Cándido. Either that, or she would hold onto the new stores and they would share the hardware store equally between them. Natalia was shaken. She rose from the sofa, and once again Cándido kissed her fingertips to contain her.

'I'm the one that's expanding the business after all. Besides, you don't have children and it'll be up to mine to look after you when you're old.'

'What children?' Do you mean that imbecile? Haven't you figured out he's a retard yet?' Natalia regretted her words immediately, because Mother pierced her with the withering look fed by the wrath that terrified them all. She sat down again and said in a low voice, by way of apology, 'Ramón isn't even named Cándido.'

Having said that, Natalia curled up on the sofa and stared at the floor, sad and disillusioned.

Whenever they argued, Mother always ended up by reminding them that when Ramón was stillborn there was no one at her side. Neither her husband nor them. No one had accompanied her to the hospital because Cándido was too busy in the hardware store and Natalia was out shopping. She told them about how she'd been loading the washing machine with dirty laundry and how her body started screaming that the time had come. She grabbed a toiletry bag into which she had piled things she would need for her personal hygiene and a little white case into which she had placed a change of clothes for herself and new, soft clothes for the baby. She got into the car and crossed the city, with the city crossing her body in half, like a rusty sword. But Mother was so strong, and such a stickler for orderliness that she had to leave the car correctly parked and in line with the other vehicles. But Mother was so brave that she walked to the reception desk, bent over, and said she was about to give birth. It was like seeing someone wounded by a gunshot to the guts trying to hold back the blood by squeezing their abdomen with their hands. They took her, her toiletry bag and her little white suitcase to a room with two other women. She was in there for too long, not able to tell if it was for one hour or twenty. When her son was born, he was wrapped in a blanket and she was asked if she was alone. She was alone. Her husband was sailing thousands of kilometers away, steering a ship along some route in the South Pacific, and what little family she did have must have been too busy, because they hadn't deigned to show up. Then she was informed that the child was stillborn. They didn't tell her this with any gentleness, with any tenderness. She was informed of this by voices that emerged from the dark mouths that inhabited bodies made of clay or mud. Mother stared at the ceiling, gutted. The emptiness that starts in her stomach when she's sad, and sucks her inward like the mouth of a vacuum cleaner, had opened up for the first time. The sadness that whirls her like a centrifuge was born. She was shot through by a pain deeper than the one that made her scream as she gave birth. She was taken to a room and told she'd be given something so she could rest. And off they went with the baby, whom they'd left on a bed, wrapped in a white blanket. A little snow baby, a puff of cotton. A piece of flesh that had fallen from her womb. Someone wanted to know the baby's name and she asked what for, since there was no longer a baby. They told her it was for the death certificate. She said his first name was Cándido. Cándido. And then, stunned, wasted, she gave the surnames. She didn't weep. She asked a nurse to dress him in the soft clothes she'd brought for him so he wouldn't be cold. Perhaps the baby was cold. Death had to be frozen and empty because that's how she felt: frozen and empty. She had just surrendered to the feverish sleep of the tranquilizers when a man entered the room and said, 'Ma'am, your son has just woken up. It's hard to believe, but it happens sometimes. The bad part is that his brain's been starved of oxygen for too long, but the boy's fine. They'll bring him over soon. He's called Cándido, right?'

Mother, about to fall asleep, answered no, that Cándido was the name of the child who had died, and that this one, the new one, could not have the same name.

'What's your name?'

'Ramón,' the man replied.

'That's a nice name, Ramón. A nice name for my son.'

Felisa entered the living room with her head hung low, holding the tray at chest level. She left the bottle of wine and the skewers on the table and ran for refuge to the kitchen, because all that had nothing to do with her. In the kitchen, employing the same magic she would use to transform an ordinary thread into beautiful embroidery, she turned the onion, the potatoes, and the eggs into a delicious tortilla. Ramón took care to squash with a fork the piece he served to the Little Girl, and then hungrily devoured the rest.

Natalia and Cándido left shortly after, in silence, cowed by the screaming of Mother, who for the umpteenth time had thrown the solitude of that day in the hospital in their faces. At that point, neither of them dared say anything.

When they quarreled, Natalia wouldn't show up at Mother's house for a while. She would phone Felisa to see what Mother's mood was like and wait for the right moment to appear with a tray of cookies and her head high, looking forwards and with her mouth dying to pour out the latest gossip overheard at the stores and café. On the Little Girl's birthday, Natalia dared to phone Mother to ask if it would be all right to give the Child a dress and some shoes. With that and her appearance mid-afternoon on Cándido's arm bearing two boxes wrapped in gift paper, she brought an end to that brief period of emptiness.

The Little Girl was now three years old, one for each candle stuck in the cream birthday cake. The Little Girl crawled under the tables looking for feet to suck. Mother grabbed her by the elastic band of her pants and slapped her for being such a pig. 'What's this business about putting your mouth around a shoe?' The Little Girl cried, but it wasn't long before she laughed, because Ramón came to her rescue and asked:

'How old's the Little Girl?'

The Little Girl counted the candles that crowned the birthday cake. Ramón had taught her to count to ten, but she was only able to count up to four. She would jump from four to seven. 'One, two, twee, fow... seven, nine. One, two, twee, fow... Ten!' She could count up to three without any trouble, so when Ramón asked her, she raised three fingers, making an effort to keep them straight and separate from the other fingers that had nothing to say. They didn't count. They were fingers trying to lower their heads and crouch against the palm of her hand. It was hard. It wasn't at all easy for the girl to control her fingers when she still didn't know the proportions of the world, and didn't know how to move her round body through it.

'The Little Girl is twee years old,' the Little Girl said merrily.

Ramón had given her a small funnel of shiny tin. He had almost certainly spirited it out of the hardware store. He opened the Little Girl's mouth, and to the amazement of Mother, the aunt and uncle, and Felisa, put the funnel in her mouth and poured a good amount of Coca-Cola into it. The girl coughed and the liquid began spilling down her cheeks and dripping down her chin. Mother shouted, 'Ramón, you're a raving nutcase!' and Felisa told him he lacked any judgment whatsoever. Cándido laughed as though watching two circus clowns. Mother became angry at Ramón, who then sat on a bench by the kitchen window, far from the celebratory table. He was quiet, but aware of his sister's tears. To make her laugh, he tied the funnel on top of his head.

'Don't do anything stupid,' cautioned Mother, pointing at him with an aggressive painted fingernail, but containing her laughter.

And he went on to do foolish things with the funnel on his head. From the countertop, he took a handful of parsley that struggled to remain green in a glass half filled with water. He placed the parsley in the funnel's narrow passage and stumbled around the kitchen, pretending to be drunk. The girl, for whom laughter and tears ran the length of a playground slide, nearly choked with laughter.

He then took her in arms, kissed her, and apologized.

'Does the Little Girl forgive me, or doesn't she forgive me?'

The Little Girl encompassed the enormous neck with her tiny arms. Meanwhile, Mother lit the candles on the cake and Natalia started clapping like a wind-up doll. Cándido was out on the balcony, smoking. It was summer, the twentieth of July, 1984. A Friday afternoon. Ramón was sixteen years old and the girl had just turned three. It was warm, but the clear sky, like a huge, dark blue anemone, promised a cool evening, lit by a dull, particularly distant moon.

Mother pulled the Little Girl away from Ramón and sat her on her knees. Neither one seemed very comfortable.

'You have to blow out the candles. You have to blow.'

'Like when you blow out matches,' Ramón insisted. His mouth filled with air and he released it little by little in the Child's face. 'You've got to do like I do. See?'

'Silly, I know how! I done it befaw,' she said, offended, angered, her face stern.

But it didn't work out the first time. Mother brought her closer to the cake and she was able to blow out one of the candles. Natalia clapped again. Felisa wore an inane smile that struck those around the table like a pink half-moon. Cándido threw his cigarette out onto the street and the still burning end traced its resigned defeat in the sky. Blowing out the next candles was harder: the candles flickered when the Little Girl blew them, they appeared to go out, but would come back again. Ramón helped her.

'All done!'

Everyone clapped. Then they ate the cake. There weren't any other children at the party, but they weren't needed. They all seemed happy as things were, discreetly happy. Even Mother smiled and stroked her daughter's golden tresses. Ramón couldn't have too much cake, so he got tired of sitting at the table and stood up. Mother put the girl on the floor, nearly brushing her off her clothes like a cake crumb. But Ramón was there waiting for her with the funnel.

'If we stick the Little Girl through here,' said Ramón, showing her the wide mouth of the funnel, 'and take her out this end, the Little Girl will come out like a sausage.'

'Don't want to! Make sausages with Mommy!' Annoyed but happy, the Little Girl twirled on her legs twice, eyes closed, picturing herself as a ballerina.

But Ramón didn't want to turn Mother into sausages, or Aunt and Uncle, or Felisa, who was watching them through blurred, suspicious eyes when he took hold of the Little Girl by the waist to keep her from hitting the table during the last twirl. He thought of something better: he took an apple, put it in the funnel's mouth, and asked the Little Girl to close her eyes. She closed them. When he told her to open them, she did. How wonderful! The apple had vanished and little colored beads were dripping from the funnel's neck. They were so shiny, so pretty, that the Little Girl's eyes burned with the fires of covetousness.

'Gimme, gimme! I'm gonna make a necklace.'

Ramón gave them to her. He always gave her everything she asked for. He would work magic with swollen hands, deposit gooey cow-tongue licks and twisted plunger kisses on her cheeks, and turn into a dromedary for her. He would cover himself in a sheet and become a ghost. He would get on all fours and turn into a lazy cat that barked instead of meowing. While the children played, the adults spoke softly or kept silent. They seemed to be waiting for something. They seemed to be anticipating some kind of miracle that would shake them – especially Mother – like fruit hanging from a tree. They waited.

Ramón and the Little Girl went all over the house, funnel in hand. The funnel swallowed a broom, swallowed the girl's tiny toothbrush, swallowed the old Kent Miller soldier who'd lost a leg long ago. When it swallowed the broom, the funnel spat out three glass balls like fish-eyes. When it swallowed the toothbrush, it spewed cologne. When it ate the crippled soldier, it dropped a disgusting bone resembling the rib of a fried chicken. Ramón convinced the girl that the funnel had given them a very important bone from the soldier's leg and that he, since he did similar work at the hardware store every day (rebuilding the arms and legs of people who had lost them in car accidents or at war), would restore the old, threadbare Kent Miller marine that the High Captain had brought him at least seven and a quarter years previously from one of his journeys.

In the kitchen the wait went on.

But the miracle didn't occur. The aunt and uncle left without making any noise and Felisa put the dirty plates in the dishwasher, wiping the marble countertop with a dry cloth. She couldn't finish cleaning the kitchen because Mother had thrown her out. She wanted to be alone, sitting at the table with a piece of half-eaten cake while staring fixedly at the phone hanging on the wall. Felisa left angrily, but before going up to her apartment she looked for the Little Girl to give her a kiss, and warned Ramón that God could see everything, even one's deepest thoughts. Ramón dropped his head, as he did whenever Felisa spoke to him of God. God must have impressive vision, even greater than that of whales. 'Some whales,' Ramón thought with his head bowed, faced with Felisa's threat of divine retribution, 'can see as far as a cat.'

'Is God a cat or a whale?' he asked aloud, seeking Mother's comfort as Felisa's heels clicked their way up the stairs leading to the attic apartment. But his mother was saying such horrible things that Ramón covered the Little Girl's ears.

'Mooooommy! Those are really ugly words!'

'So what?' She shuddered down the dregs of cava in the bottoms of the cups and furiously extinguished a cigarette on a cake-stained plate. 'What do you know about it? Your father is a damned son of a bitch…'

Ramón took the Little Girl to her room. He looked for her pajamas under the pillow and changed her. He held the funnel to her ear and told her some of his fantasy-ridden stories through the shiny tin object. The concentrated air emerging from the funnel's neck tickled her ear. The Little Girl enjoyed the tickles, liked Ramón's distorted voice, and liked the tender smell emanating from his embrace. And amid these pleasures, the Little Girl fell asleep.

She slept and dreamed that a cherry-colored beam of light came in through the slats of the Venetian blind.

Many tiny people walked along the beam of light, legless soldiers and brooms that swept in birthday cakes. The beam of light doubled up to form the number eight. The people walking along the beam of light would bump into each other forever. They could walk it a million times and always meet on that road that could be traveled from above and below. At first they didn't even greet each other, but sat down to eat the strawberry cake on which three lit candles were sparkling. They looked like happy people until they began turning into funnels with arms and legs. They fought to gobble each other up. And they did gobble each other up. In the end, all that was left was a big, fat, shiny funnel. Then after millions of turns along the strip, the damned funnel found a way to reach the Little Girl and drink her like a malted milkshake.

The Little Girl woke up afraid. She got out of bed and walked in the dark to Ramón's room. There was no one in bed, the blinds were up, the geranium looked concerned, and the old one-legged soldier looked mournfully at her from the carpet. She felt sorry for Kent Miller, but knew that Ramón had one of his bones and would build a new leg for him at the hardware store the next day. She left Ramón's room and walked past the kitchen. There was no one in the kitchen. In the corridor she tripped over the body of the broom lying on the floor. At the end of the corridor she saw the door to Mother's room ajar and the light on. She ran toward it, calling for Ramón. She saw Mother's body in the bed and Ramón beside her, and even discerned Ramón's final stroke on that head consumed by a conflagration of red hair. When he heard the Little Girl's voice, he put on his blue-and-white-striped bathrobe and ran out. He was confused. He picked her up in his arms, sang her a lullaby with a slow rhythm that only repeated the movements of his enormous heart, and put her back to bed.

'My little darling, who would take care of you if Ramón weren't here?' The liquid, marine-like voice that burst into bubbles and then into mighty jets from the depths of his lungs succeeded in putting her to sleep. 'Who would take care of Mommy?'

The Little Girl let herself be tucked in, still shaken by the last echo of a sensual sob. Ramón bent over to kiss her on the forehead with a warm, soporific kiss. But as his mouth approached hers, the Little Girl felt the smell of a breath that wasn't Ramón's.

It was Mother's breath.

Matías, the doorman, phoned them mid-morning. Ramón had long ago woken the Little Girl, had dressed her and was waiting nervously for Mother to get out of bed. He'd even prepared a small suitcase with the girl's and his clothes and left it on the yellow velvet upholstered armchair in the foyer. But Mother wasn't getting up. She woke up when the phone rang. It was ten thirty. Matías told her that her brother was waiting downstairs in the car.

'Tell them to park and come upstairs,' she answered, hanging up the phone.

Shortly after, the elevator deposited the aunt and uncle on the doormat. Ramón opened the door with the Little Girl holding onto his neck. Natalia asked if they'd had lunch and Ramón said they hadn't. Cándido looked at the clock, made a gesture of exasperation, and decided to wait in the living room. Natalia made them breakfast while Mother dressed in her room and hurriedly gathered up some clothing for the weekend. Mother entered the kitchen just as the coffee pot began to expel the fragrant smell of coffee and, without looking to either side, filled a glass to the brim and drank it almost in a single gulp. She didn't look at anyone. Ramón expected at least an affectionate look, some gesture of complicity, but Mother wasn't even aware of his presence.

'Would you like crackers or buttered toast?' he asked Mother, trying to remain a lover and a confidant even while offering food.

'Where's Felisa?' she asked, and Ramón knew he'd better keep quiet. That his duty at that moment was to be invisible. 'Just look at this kitchen!'

'What happened yesterday? Did he call in the end?' Natalia inquired.

'Like hell he did! It's tragic he didn't even remember his daughter's birthday.' Mother leaned against the wall tiles, putting on a resigned expression. 'What does it matter? He hasn't even had the decency to come meet her.'

The remains of the birthday dinner had been left on the table, remains that Felisa had been unable to pick up because she, Mother, had thrown her out of the house. Natalia finished making the children's breakfast and hurriedly cleared the table, especially of the remains of alcohol and cigarettes. Mother took a last sip of her coffee and vanished. She reappeared more or less half an hour later, renewed, wearing a bright yellow dress and with a travel bag in her hand.

'Come on, let's be off.'

And they were off. Some weekends they would go to the aunt and uncle's villa, which, between the house and the land, took up a small hillside at the entrance to the city, Everyone liked that house because of its garden and its swimming pool, and because Mother would free herself of her almost continuous bad mood and smile. Even clothing that appeared lackluster in the city seemed brighter there, in the country, as bright as the fruit in the vegetable garden, like the tomatoes and peas. She would even play with the Little Girl and wasn't constantly worried whether or not Ramón had put on his bib to eat. The Little Girl's appetite would be roused as soon as her feet touched the grass. Her stomach wasn't constrained as it was in the city. Since Mother seemed calm and even pleased, the painful plug that blocked the pit of the Little Girl's stomach vanished as well, and her throat would open with the desire to swallow the light, the rain, the dogs and even the presence of Natalia, who sought out the shadows to stay out of the sun. If it was winter and raining, they would stay in the house, mesmerized by the fire, or on the porch, enjoying the small puddles left by the dogs as they came in and shook themselves. If it was hot, they would spend hours by the pool: Ramón had spent years waiting for the metamorphosis that would turn him into a whale, and his intuition told him this could only happen in water. In the water. Breathing water. In the pool.

As soon as they arrived, the Little Girl fell face forward in the garden and got a mouthful of dirt. She felt a warm fluid flowing from her forehead down to her mouth. It tasted sweet. Or salty. It tasted hot. Tears and mucus soon joined the blood and soil, and the Little Girl felt as if she had a mouthful of mud and bubbles. Mother took her into her arms, and for a second the girl felt she was floating. With one hand, Mother clutched her against her breast and lifted her head with the other. She extracted a tissue from her handbag, spat into it, and wiped off the Little Girl's forehead and cheeks.

'Yessir. Spit is a good antibiotic, among the best,' Cándido remarked, just as Ramón was beginning to look repulsed.

'She's cracked her head open,' he yelled nervously. 'How disgusting! The Little Girl's going to die!'

No one paid Ramón any attention; no one asked him what disgust had to do with death. He fluttered around the blood like an anguished dog. Cándido approached the girl and began to riffle through her hair to see if she had an open, bleeding crack. All she had was a small wound on her brow, but it bled copiously. Ramón, frightened, wanted to take the girl out of Mother's arms and away from her uncle's devotion. Mother sat down and the Little Girl allowed herself to fall placidly into her lap. Mother asked Natalia for some peroxide and cotton and dabbed the liquid gently on the open wound. It hurt.

'It's nothing,' said Cándido, calming her with his slow, patient words. 'These kids are made of rubber.'

The Little Girl stopped crying. She opened her tear-filled eyes and saw her brother's head hovering above her, under a cloud scurrying across the sky. She felt dizzy when she looked up and closed her eyes again. She didn't take long to open them again: Ramón's head still floated over her face like a balloon fastened to a hand by a fishing line. The feeling that her brother was constantly floating, that he was able to float up to the clouds if someone in the family stopped paying him attention, would remain with the Little Girl all her life.

Surprised, she regarded Ramón's round, pale face looking like a mass of raw dough. He stuck his tongue out at her, tickled her tummy, and the Little Girl laughed again. When she opened her mouth, her teeth still spat out soil from the garden.

The aunt and uncle's villa was a pleasant place from which one could see the tall buildings bordering the coastline. The house was surrounded by a considerable acreage full of trees, and beyond the garden, Cándido had cleared a patch of wilderness in which he grew all manner of vegetables. There were two dogs: one named Bruce and the other Lee. Bruce was a black-coated German Shepherd and Lee was an old mongrel with brown and white spots. Ramón enjoyed playing with the dogs and helping the uncle chop wood or cultivate the terrain. Mother didn't concern herself with him at all, because she knew that all the physical effort he engaged in over the weekend would serve as a natural tranquilizer for a couple of days.

Natalia did no work on the farm. She only looked after the garden flowers and collected the vegetables when they were ready to be harvested. She enjoyed the feel of the tomatoes, the peas, the beans and the peppers when she pulled them off the vine and placed them in a wicker basket. She felt laden with abundance, like when she'd been cooking and filled plastic containers with roast veal, stuffed chicken, tomato or apple sauce. And when she made pastries and the kitchen smelled of marmalade and caramelized sugar, she felt complete. It felt good to walk among that abundance of food, but above all she enjoyed admiring the beautiful ingredients for recipes she would get from magazines or receive from a friend. She caressed them. She caressed the round pork loins before marinating them in garlic, oil, and parsley. She caressed the bodies of the chickens that would be slightly pink after she burnt off the persistent fuzz that clung to their skin after they were scalded, and she would hold them close to her nose. Once they'd been plucked, Natalia would pour a small quantity of moonshine into a dish, set it alight and then slowly pass the chicken over the blue flames. When she touched the chickens, when she smelled them, it was as if she were stroking the body of a newborn that smiled at her, naked, with open arms and legs and a swollen belly, lying on the polished granite countertop. Mother said that cooking gave Natalia a pleasure similar to that of taking care of a baby. It could not be said, however, that she was particularly demonstrative toward Ramón or the Little Girl. She did not caress them with the same tenderness she reserved for a rack of calf ribs or the rough skin of a potato. No. Never. She looked at them, especially when she was alone with them, with a sort of hatred mixed with jealousy, and it was quite possible that after the children had left her side, she would contain those feelings in one of the jars of marmalade, or freeze them like the dishes of food she arranged – suitably labeled – at the back of the freezer.

When it was very hot, Natalia would keep the blinds half shut so that the house remained cool. Mother and Ramón sought the darkness of the living room during siesta time to avoid the scorching July sun. There was an enormous piece of furniture in the room, an armoire that must have been born and raised in the living room, as it had adapted perfectly to the wall and the shape of the ceiling. Along its upper section it appeared to want to bend forward, like a plant growing inside a house that collides with the categorical, wretched refusal by the ceiling to open a pathway for it toward the light. From within the armoire, and through the beveled glass of the doors could be seen small flashes of stemware, bright challenges to the opacity of the dust compelled to remain on the outer side of the glass. The armoire wasn't ugly. It was made of oak and was at least a hundred years old, and had the elegance of an elderly gentleman compelled to trim the hair sprouting from his nostrils and ears. At least that was what Ramón replied when Mother asked him to describe that piece of furniture that presided over the living room.

'He's a portly, elegant old man, with a hat and bow tie. His eyes sparkle because he drinks malt whisky and smokes Havana cigars. He smells very good, of sandalwood. He trims his nostril and ear hair with little scissors, like the ones Felisa uses to cut embroidery thread.'

'And where do you see his bow tie?' Mother inquired, proud of the boy's imagination but endeavoring, as always, to keep his head anchored in reality. It was Mother who most anxiously sought the invisible thread that tied Ramón to the ground.

'But Mommy! Don't be silly! Can't you see his bow tie?' He got up from the sofa and his immense body opened a dark, mobile hole in the armoire. 'This is the bow tie, right under his head and his hat.'

Mother finally managed to see the bow tie. It turned out to be an oval-shaped alpaca tray resting against the dark recesses of the armoire, gradually growing narrower from the middle. Exactly the opposite of a bow tie, but the answer was good. It would do. She then tried to see the head and the hat, but that was impossible now. Not that it mattered. It was a game to Ramón, and all she had to do was write down his words in a tortoiseshell-covered log that was actually a photo album her husband had brought back from some now-distant journey. It had been one of Ramón's teachers from his school days who'd advised her to do it, and she did it lovingly, with a passionate devotion toward her son. When she'd spent several months writing down definitions – several a month, and there were still some twenty pages left to finish the log – it occurred to her to write a title on the first page, which she had left blank by some miraculous intuition: *Anthology of Quotidian Objects*. It came to her as she was poring over catalogs of appliances and furniture to choose merchandise for the first stores. Those catalogs of objects were, in fact, like the poetry anthologies she enjoyed reading. She liked the word 'anthology': it seemed important and poetic, and she thought it suited the book in which she gathered Ramón's definitions of the objects that shared his life. Under the title she wrote 'Ramón,' with no surnames or anything. It didn't need them.

After writing down Ramón's new definition, she lit a cigarette. She thought the title was beautiful, and her lips even quivered with emotion at the thought of having been able to create something pretty. That wounding flicker of beauty gave her the certainty that this book that Ramón was dictating to her would be the most beautiful thing she would ever do in her life, and she was just three years shy of turning forty. And with some twenty pages still blank. She was so distracted by meditating on the title of the log and smoking to feed that insight that she wasn't aware that Ramón was staring fixedly at her breasts. He approached her, took her hand and placed it between his legs. Mother's hand recoiled, seeking shelter between her back and the sofa when she noticed her son's erection. She looked from side to side, afraid that someone might be watching them.

'Not now, honey,' she said, noticing how the boy's mouth was asking wordlessly for help, and how his eyes, boring down to the depths of the womb where he was conceived, were clouded by the need to satisfy an urgent desire.

'I've got to do it, Mommy.' Ramón's voice, the mountain crowned by a sweet, childish cotton cloud, was about to turn into a volcano and disgorge its irrepressible white lava.

'Go to the bathroom and lock the door on the inside,' Mother said, snuffing out her cigarette as she got up and walked him to the door. 'You don't have to ask me for permission every time.'

She stood by the door, making sure no one was approaching. She knew too well the sounds of her son's most intimate ceremony, and knew it barely lasted a minute. She recalled that when Ramón was younger, he'd thought to do it in front of Natalia, who screamed, outraged, that the boy was a damned ape in heat. Immaculate, exquisite, and elegant, Natalia didn't consider Ramón a human being. At most he was a baby in a man's body, and babies were asexual beings to her. Sexless angels, innocent souls dancing in limbo like dust motes cavorting in a sunbeam. Mother had to teach him that satisfying desire was a personal thing, and that he couldn't do it in front of others because it made them uncomfortable. Earlier, she had taught him how to calm it down and how to clean up afterwards. She even allowed him – on more than one occasion – to lie beside her and touch her. But that was an unutterable secret, something that tormented her every time it happened, and no matter how much she loved him, she felt soiled, debilitated, and weighed down at the mere thought that the touch of her son's hands could bring her any kind of pleasure.

Mother waited outside the door until she knew it was over, and waited still longer to hear the muffled water from the shower falling on Ramón's body. Suddenly, the living room and the end of the corridor were filled with the Little Girl's screams and Natalia's voice promising to read her a story if she quieted down. The Little Girl angrily told her to leave her alone. Mother quit her sentry duty in front of the bathroom and walked down the corridor thinking that those hysterical screams could only be quieted by sinking the Little Girl in a barrel of fuel and setting it on fire.

'I think she's hungry,' Natalia said when Mother looked in. 'She wanted a cookie and I didn't give her one.'

Mother recomposed her facial expression so the Little Girl wouldn't realize that only seconds ago she'd wanted to roast her alive, and walked into the living room with a face that was a mixture of fatigue and contempt. She was unable to display a minimal amount of tenderness when Natalia handed the Little Girl over to her and the Little Girl clung to her neck. Mother accepted her and allowed the Child to rest her head against her shoulder. She didn't even bother to pat the girl repeatedly on the back as Natalia and Ramón did to calm her down. She held her in her arms, and that was sufficient. The Little Girl wept, and, accustomed to receiving nothing from Mother beyond the smell of her body and the sound of her heartbeats, she settled down.

'Why don't you grow up already?' Mother wondered aloud. Ignoring Natalia's rebukes, she sat on the sofa with the Little Girl holding onto her neck and lit a cigarette. She leaned back, tired. 'I wish you'd been born when you were at least twenty.'

Perhaps hurt by Mother's cruel words, the Little Girl slid down to the floor. She walked over to a corner of the carpet lit by the sun, and stood there playing with the dust dancing among the sunbeams, embracing her belly with her chubby arms full of milk and tiny pieces of meat and vegetables. Mother made herself comfortable against the curve of the sofa. The air was so still that she could smell the clean scent of lavender soap opening the bathroom door. The Little Girl also noticed it and turned to face the corridor. Her expression of annoyance fell away and morphed into exultant hope. When she spotted Ramón at the door, she tried to get up, but began to rock from side to side and fell back into a sitting position. Ramón picked her up and threw her into the air. The Little Girl laughed again. Mother began tapping her forehead with the tips of all ten fingers at the same time.

Seeing Ramón with his lust quenched, cuddling the Little Girl, caused an enormous rent in her body. The fibers of her virgin silk dress opened and displayed the movements of thousands of worms producing the delicate threads that had woven the yellow cloth she wore. They displayed the entrails of beauty, the simple embroidery out of which death is woven.

At noon on Sunday, while Natalia prepared lunch and Cándido patched up a hose in the shade of the porch, Ramón and the Little Girl were playing at the edge of the pool and Mother sunning herself. There, in that space filled with light, all the regulations that corseted them into the rigidity of daily city life, where it was necessary to maintain order, whatever the cost, were broken. There, without the perpetual watchfulness of Felisa or Mother, Ramón and the Little Girl dove into the water and pretended to be fish and algae, to touch each other without the unhealthy gaze of the babysitter who accused them of being sinners for loving each other so much, for caressing each other in secret places. There, in the water of the swimming pool that hot Sunday noon, occurred Ramón's joyful transformation into a whale. Only he didn't swim through the air or flush himself down the drainpipe – he was stunned, staring at the sky, under the sky-blue water.

'Look, look! That's how whales are born!' Ramón shouted, making a fish face and going 'bop-bop' before taking a headlong leap into the pool.

Mother heard the thunderous sound in the water, got out of the hammock and walked toward the pool. She saw

Ramón's body as it sank, striking the tiles decorated with little blue dolphins that adorned the floor of the pool. She waited at the edge, paralyzed, with the Little Girl at her side. She waited a long time until she was certain her son would never move again, and finally, with a hoarse shout, she cried out to Cándido. Cold and expressionless, she abandoned to the water's embrace the person who had finally given meaning to the ten fingers on her hands, the joints of her bones, and the tenderness which, at some distant moment, had solidified in her womb.

Felisa and the Little Girl walked into the apartment. They felt a heavy sadness prowling up and down the long corridor, pausing at the closed doors of the bedrooms. A yellow light advanced through the kitchen window, encroaching on the penumbra that distressed the apartment. The Little Girl, startled, seized the nanny's hand as she looked down the corridor and with her eyes wide open made sure that all was still. Despite how deeply she missed him, she wished the door to Ramón's room would remain locked. The tone of the light reminded Felisa of old memories of dry straw, and she realized it had been many years since she'd mowed hay. The warm fragrance of straw linked her to recollections of the joyful satisfaction of a fevered body after the reaping was done, and she convinced herself that this was a good memory – pasty, sticky, imbued with desire – with which to open the doors leading to the corridor. With the Little Girl clutching her hand, she entered the kitchen to open the window and let in one of those gentle August breezes that enter with a purifying, calming effect on all manner of pains. She then went into the living room and saw that the TV set was on, and that a cigarette had burned through in the glass ashtray. She closed the box in which Mother kept her cigarettes and dragged the Little Girl to a large room, seldom used since it was furnished as a dining room and no large dinners or special events had been held there, at least not while Felisa had been in the house. It was a shame to keep it closed all the time, because the furniture was truly beautiful and she took care to wax and polish it at least a couple of times every year. Beyond the table and before one reached the window covered in heavy velveteen drapes, there was a charming lacquered Chinese credenza that the High Captain had brought back from one of his voyages. There was also a very fine, delicate carpet and a low table surmounted by a large porcelain jar, and also a pair of easy chairs upholstered in cherry-colored chintz. Mother was sitting – or, more precisely, hiding – in an area of the rug free of table legs, like a snail under the unbearable weight of a painful cuirass. The credenza's doors and drawers were open. Sadly and tearfully, Mother was tearing up letters and photographs. Small piles of onion-skin paper and little pieces of broken bodies had formed on the carpet. Father's anatomy had been thoroughly drawn and quartered. To her side, within reach of her hand, as if ensuring them protection, she placed the photos and letters she had decided to keep.

The letters would be stored later on in the dresser in her bedroom with her underwear, but the photos would remain forever trapped in the box, inside the credenza and the dining room almost always in shadow.

'Are you all right, Ma'am?' Felisa dared to ask. Mother shot her through with a look filled with wrath and sorrow. She was about to say something, but when she saw the Little Girl, she decided to remain quiet and return to her self-involved task.

Felisa took the Little Girl by the hand, dragging her out of the room. She took her to the living room and sat her in front of the TV set. She had turned three in July, and for a long time – months now – it had been hard to ignore her questions.

'What did they do to Mommy?

'Mommy's sad, Little Girl.'

'Why is she sad?'

Ramón's dilemmas entered her mind and she waited for the Little Girl to add a second option to the question. She waited, alert, looking for the yellow color of dry straw in the light pouring into the living room as a source of courage. But the girl wasn't Ramón, and asked again, 'Why is she sad?' Felisa's reply, however, was similar to one she would have given the boy:

'I'm going to bring you your afternoon snack.'

As soon as the nanny was gone, the Little Girl climbed off the sofa and went to the place where she'd seen Mother. She tiptoed toward the door, and on tiptoe managed to open the door. She advanced stealthily: her steps were like a breeze muffled in feathers. She went in and looked.

She merely looked, merely tried to understand. The Little Girl had been observing her for a long time when Mother turned her head. That was the first time the Little Girl saw the dark monster crawling out of Mother's mouth, a monster that would have devoured her had it not been for Felisa entering the dining room, looking around for her, holding the tea tray in her hand. Felisa lifted her into the air and saved her, by a hair's breadth, from the impact of the vase aimed straight at her head. The vase shattered noiselessly on the carpet. Felisa was flooded with the memory of young blood spilt on the hay, and felt a knot in the pit of her stomach.

As time passed, the Little Girl would remember Mother cutting herself to pieces on the dining-room floor.

But the impact of the vase against the floor was so painful that the Child decided to forget it.

III

THE BUCKET AFTER THE ROPE

In the house of a hanged man one shouldn't say the rope came after the bucket.

Amos Oz

It was eleven o'clock at night in the city. It was two in the afternoon in the Bay and also in San Diego when Angela picked up the phone and answered with a distant 'What's up, my girl?' Despite 'my girl' seeming to be affectionate, the tone of Angela's voice was clearly intended to brush me off with a frosty efficaciousness that hurt me. She replied to my questions in monosyllables and wasn't in the least bit concerned about me. She was angry, very angry, and had her reasons: I hadn't even bothered to send her a text message, hadn't written her any emails after promising that I would send her one a day so she would feel me close to her. And during that phone call I was incapable of asking for forgiveness or being polite, not even a little bit. We were two slabs of granite trying to converse with each other: sparks flew from the friction, and sharp corners emerged, when what I needed, for once, were soft recesses of tenderness. Angela was cruel.

'Sorry, girl, I've got a fucking pile of work to do.' She spoke to me in English deliberately, to exclude me from her affection, drawing out the 'fucking' to make the point that I couldn't just interrupt her whenever it suited me. She had a fucking pile of work to do. A fucking pile of work.

'Take care.' Diffident and cowed, I said goodbye in English as well. But I don't think she heard me, as I could no longer hear her on the other end of the phone when I said it.

I was sad because I hated the selective manner in which Angela used language and because I hated my inability to ask for help. I took the cellphone and crushed it as I told myself a thousand times that I was an imbecile and a goddamned egotist. I was in the park, and the darkness of the trees and the sky, diluted in the yellow lamplight, made me feel nostalgic for light and color. I needed light and color like I needed, at that very moment, the alluring shadow of the benches nailed in the twists and turns of the park. I sought out one and sat by a fountain, far from the lights. I bent over my abdomen in a gesture that reminded me of Mother and, as I'd done many times before, chased it away, trying to evoke the sea at the Bay, or the summer trips that had taken me to places that had made me happy. From Florence to Cairo, from the cold of Patagonia to the primordial soup of Varanasi. From Kathmandu to the salt flats of Uyuni. Constant travel was my greatest pleasure. Getting on a plane and feeling that I'd freed myself of who I was, of what had concerned me between one trip and the next, was my most cherished liberty. Filling myself with new sounds, smells and tastes everywhere I went was for me the most satisfying way to grow.

I despised recognizing Mother's traits in myself. I would correct my posture constantly when I sat, with my head tilted backward, like her. I'd be infuriated when, faced with a plate of food, I found myself holding cutlery in the same way she did, as if feeding were a bothersome imposition. I also identified her in the way we both held our cigarettes, allowing our worn-out fingers to sag under the weight of the smoke with more exhaustion than if we were each carrying a marble column. I discovered her within me, but she wasn't with me, and I was increasingly weakened by the permanent pretense of erasing any trace of her in my body and personality. I was afraid, of course, of turning into her.

As I was sitting on the park bench, the fountain sang me a gentle lullaby. I could see young couples walking by, holding each other by the waist, stopping to kiss and unaware of my presence. A dog approached me, wagging its tail in such an exaggerated manner that it looked as if it were swimming. It licked my shoes. I gazed at it: it was just a pup wanting to play. I stroked its head and it returned my interest with a long, yellow stare that took me away from the yellow lamplight and returned me to the gloom of Mother's room. The dog seemed happier than me, and told me so with a lick of its tongue like a compassionate smile on my hands, and it went away without further ado, hearing the voice of a woman calling after it.

'Piti! Piti! Come here, Piti!' The woman was only a few meters away, holding onto the puppy's leash and gently slapping it against her legs. I didn't notice at first, but when the dog jumped on her, lighting her up with its splendid black fur, I saw that the woman was wearing carpet slippers and pajamas under her threadbare housecoat. She looked at me, perhaps surprised at seeing me alone in the dark. She said goodbye to me by lifting the leash in the air while the dog scratched away at other feet walking along the path.

The woman went away, but the sign she made with the leash floated in the air for a while, bringing to mind Angela and her unending love. Her love was that of an explorer intent on rummaging inside me to find something that didn't exist. I wasn't a vine concealing bunches of grapes overlooked by the vintner. Despite her failures, she persisted in exploring me until I gave up and lied, just to make her happy. Just to have found a grain of something, I would invent it and offer it to her, also happy to be able to do it. I'd lied to her so many times that I didn't feel guilty anymore. I'd lied to her in desire, in pleasure, in my devotion for her. I gave myself to her because when I met her she was stronger than me, and knew how to bend me to her will, how to dominate me, how to make me lower my head and accept her without question.

I had met her three years earlier in La Paz, on a postgraduate course in the south of Baja California. I had just arrived at the Bay and was spending all the time I had chasing gray whales. I lived in proud self-sufficiency and was permanently and unconsciously haughty. I had already traveled enough to know that whenever I boarded a plane, I managed to shed all the excess luggage. I had a surplus of sadness, a surplus of pain, unpleasant thoughts slid off my body like fake skin as I rose meters and meters into the sky. When I saw her for the first time, I don't know if it was her voice or her age – she can't have been more than a few years older than me – or the confidence with which she moved her hands, or her horsey look full of edges that appealed to me under simple, unfussy clothing – shorts, leather sandals, black tops fastened to her shoulders with ties, exposing the softness of her belly – or her long tresses, as black and dry as a powerful, wild mane... I don't know what it was, but I was unable to prevent myself from peppering her with absolutely inane questions to draw her attention. My classmates were upset, she grew increasingly annoyed as the days went by and I kept up the questioning, and I would even tidy myself up before entering her class. There was something about that woman that attracted me, and I couldn't help it.

And all she talked about was jellyfish. But she displayed them with such passion and beauty that in the end I stopped trying to encourage her and remained quiet at the back of the classroom. Silent, almost hidden, feeling a certain shame for the insolence with which I had called attention to myself during the first few classes. For days and weeks I surrendered myself to the admiration of those liquid beings that gave shape and color to my retinas, bewitched by the instructor's wonderful voice, her wisdom and joyful presence. And by the looks she aimed in my direction, wondering why I hadn't kept asking questions, knowing that I'd already given up and that I wasn't going to put up any resistance to her passion. Or to mine.

'You have a fucking problem, my girl,' she told me one night over glasses of tequila, 'and a strange look in your eyes.'

'So what are you going to do about it?' I inquired. She laughed. Because she was large, smart, and superior, and was able to laugh at an infatuated student.

'About what? The look in your eyes, or your problem?'

This made me tense, astonished, and I remained silent again, acknowledging defeat. She stroked my neck. She stroked my neck and I felt defeated, as I had felt defeated when as a child I attended the rich kids' school and couldn't sit down. I couldn't sit down. I didn't feel like sitting at the school desk just because someone had asked me to do so, kindly or menacingly. I've always found it impossible to obey direct orders that go against the grain for me, or against my need to move forward or backward. Or against the self-imposition of remaining standing, no matter how hard I am obliged to take a seat.

'Sit down!'

'No!'

'I'm telling you to sit down!'

'I don't want to!'

Even if my feet were exploding, even if I'd been slapped in the midst of the terrified silence of the other children, I would never sit down if the teacher ordered me to. I'm not entirely sure of the reason for my obsession about standing for hours, while the other students hated me for making them live though unnecessary stress. But that's what I was like: I'd remain as stiff as a board, as tense as a bow, with my teeth clenched, fighting the urge to run off in search of the protection of my brother, who'd been dead for years. I would sometimes repeat the word 'Mommy' to bolster my resolve. 'Mommy, Mommy, Mommy.' I repeated it with the same restful cadence of a mantra with which Felisa prayed the rosary before she went to bed, aware that I would never obtain an amenable response to the only prayer I knew how to say: 'Mommy, Mommy, Mommy.'

I peed myself once out of sheer pride, because I just didn't feel like asking the teacher for leave to go to the toilet. It was far more humiliating for me to ask permission to do something than to hear the laughter and derogatory remarks of my classmates as they watched the trickle of urine soaking my feet clad in black patent leather. Fine, delicate shoes of black patent leather. The teacher didn't hit me that day. I think she knew I wouldn't lower my gaze, no matter how much she hit me. She also knew I wasn't going to cry, and refrained because of that. But precisely because she didn't hit me, I cried on account of the tenderness I felt, and the tears rolled down my cheeks like streams of caustic soda. They hurt. They hurt and left marks I am still able to see and feel when I look at myself in a mirror or when I place my fingertips, all ten of them, on my face.

Staring at me while the children laughed, the teacher approached extremely cautiously, as if walking along the top of a high, narrow wall, a wet and slippery wall. I was about to hurl myself into the void as I watched her, the teacher, step confidently – very confidently – toward me, absolutely sure about what she was doing. Those steps took her across the narrow surface of the wall upon which I had perched for years and which, over time, came to be the only space separating me from a precipice. The teacher didn't embrace me or anything of that sort… it would have been terrible if she had. She merely placed her hand on the nape of my neck and began to caress it, bite it with her fingertips, press it with the palm of her hand until I let my head drop and surrendered without further resistance. Without any kind of resistance: to lying down, sitting, or walking backward or forward.

I don't know what the children did while the teacher stroked the nape of my neck. The most probable thing would be that they stopped laughing; if they'd kept laughing, I couldn't have cared less, since I felt protected by a compact layer of cotton and couldn't hear anything beyond the rustling of my hair in the teacher's hands, the sound of my flesh yielding like soft putty, and the nervous laughter of my bones at finally being released from their self-imposed rigidity. At last I'd managed to come down from the top of the wall from which I'd forbidden myself to descend until that moment. From what I can remember, it was as if someone had bested me for the first time. And it wasn't a catastrophe or anything similar. I found it delightful to yield to the caresses and to feel the inexplicable pleasure of wanting to belong to someone and surrender to their will.

The woman and the puppy passed by me again. The dog leapt toward me in search of one last stroke. The woman called to him.

'Piti! Piti! Come along, Piti!' and he ran toward the woman, who showed me the leash once again in a cheerful farewell.

I took out the phone. The time was midnight at the park and three in the afternoon in San Diego when Angela answered. I knew a triumphant smile was forming on her lips.

'What do you want me to say to you now? What do you want me to do?' I asked. I began to walk, my spirits rising to the sound of Angela's voice, which had recovered the tenderness she'd denied me during the first call, and abandoned the park, leaving behind the disconcerting sensation of absolute solitude that had overwhelmed me when she addressed me in English. I went up to the apartment with my friend's voice tingling in my ear. I went into Mother's room. Mother was asleep and Angela said she missed me.

The next day, still enveloped in a longing for my lover, Uncle Cándido insisted that I should accompany him to the villa.

'I've got to make sure there's water in the well,' he told me. 'And you can take a dip, too. It's so hot we're going to melt.'

Felisa and Aunt Natalia had taken over the house, obsessed with the opening of windows and the housekeeping, and they compelled me to go with my uncle.

'There's food in the fridge,' Natalia said as we left. 'Cándido already knows how to use a microwave.'

Uncle Cándido was a lot like Ramón, at least physically. In his naiveté as well as his wisecracks. Only he wasn't insane and had worn his name around his neck since birth. He was a thrifty sort, laid back, completely uninterested in strife. I had never gotten to know him very well because I had been raised among the women, a space in which he was an intruder that interrupted conversations, and he had no interest in participating in household discussions. Furthermore, he never discussed the gossip picked up at the hardware store like Ramón used to do, not lending it much credence and forgetting it. Ever since Mother had locked herself in her room, he was somewhat concerned because he'd been compelled to hire a company to manage the stores, another thing Mother wasn't aware of. He'd even thought about selling them and only keeping the hardware store, but Natalia was opposed to this and wasn't sure if this could be done without Mother's consent. Mother would never have agreed, and had set that down in her will.

'I can't do this, Little Girl,' he told me as we crossed the city, his eyes glued to the windshield, because he was an awful driver. 'You can see the state things are in.'

'Aunt told me that if I don't sign I'll be cut out of the will.'

'That's your mother's doing, not mine. Your aunt shouldn't have told you anything.'

We drove in silence to the villa. He turned on the radio, lowered the window, and devoted himself to the delicate task of controlling the steering wheel until we reached the top of the hill. He reached for the remote control and opened the enormous, green wrought-iron gate. He parked inside, very near the porch.

'What about the dogs?'

'What dogs?

'Bruce and Lee,' I replied, not very sure of what I was saying. He thought for a few minutes and then laughed foolishly, like Ramón.

'You're right. Bruce and Lee! They've been buried under the tomato stand for years.'

We got out of the car. Cándido, obese, moved by rubbing one thigh against the other and entered the house. I stayed in the garden. The garden was the same, but looked different – older, more tired. Grass grew in places that Natalia would not have permitted only a few years ago. Unpruned rose bushes cluttered the paths; roses shed their petals, sad and weighed down by the burden of neglect. The apple trees, however, were festooned with still-green apples, and the peach trees had new fruit, certain to ripen. The tomatoes, beans, carrots, and lettuces were as carefully arranged as the little boxes in the hardware store. In one corner of the property a group of flowering garlic plants gave a tinge of purple to the exuberant abundance.

'Have you noticed that I'm also growing beets, spinach, leeks and artichokes?' Uncle inquired as he walked toward the well. 'I'm also trying asparagus, turmeric and ginger. I've got turnips, rosemary, rue, basil, chicory, tomato cherries and winter strawberries. I should quit hardware and set up a fruit shop.'

'The fruit garden's beautiful. But the flower garden's a bit withered.'

'That's your aunt's doing!' he shouted from a corner of the vegetable garden, where the well rose amid a clearing in the grass, wilted by the merciless summer sun. 'Your aunt's getting old. It's hard to get her out of the city.'

When I caught up with him, he had already lifted the rusty iron lid that covered the well. I was going to say something, but he gestured me to keep quiet. He brought an ear close to the well's edge and listened. Satisfied with what he'd heard, he grabbed the bucket and let it drop inside, sliding the rope tied to it into the dark, cool, stone-lined throat with great care. We waited for a moment, a brief one, as brief as three of our own breaths, until the bucket made the happy sound of contact with water. Uncle Cándido smiled with satisfaction and waited.

'Would you like to pull?' He handed me the rope, but I declined. He thanked me with a slight smile and bent forward with the effort of drawing the water up to the air. When the bucket reached the stone rim, Uncle Cándido dunked his face into the water to feel and taste it. I did the same, and drank as if I'd never consumed anything so delicious. Contact with the cool, clean water inspired a sudden joy in me, an unexpected reason to stay. I had found a clearing in the stormy sky, a handhold at the bottom of the abyss. A moment of doubt, at least. But he took care to dispel it.

We strolled among the flowering pale pink turmeric, the tomatoes about to erupt into their red beauty, the fresh, aromatic laurels, the parsley in the fullness of its fertility, the potatoes and onions peering through the soil to show their pallid faces. Near the wall filled with blossoming passion flowers – which I enjoyed eating as a child when they were sprouts, and also when they opened and I could pull out their purple filaments to devour whole, sweet and meaty – Uncle asked me to sign the contract. I was shocked, and the same fear I'd experienced when Aunt Natalia had announced the intention to disown me climbed up my thighs one more.

'Sign the contract and go.' He remained silent for a while, stroking the thin stem of flowering garlic, crowned by an enormous purple and white flower. 'Your mother doesn't have to know. I couldn't care less about the business. All I want is this wonderful vegetable garden. I'll harvest the fruit and give it to the customers who've been buying from the hardware store all their lives.' He suddenly turned to look at me, elated, fully convinced about the proposal he was making. 'Sign the contract and go, then come back a couple of times a year, because there's no need for you to vanish forever. If you don't sign, let me assure you that you'll be left with nothing. You'll be left without a pension and that'll be the end of the good life for you. This is what your mother has decided.'

He kept talking while he felt the tomatoes, brought his nose close to the chicory, or admired the health of the peppers. That was how I learned how painful it is to invest such passion in your work. Because you have no choice, in the end, but to leave the fruit in alien hands, hands that are unaware of those moments of extreme loneliness, painful family arguments, renouncing a life without conflicts, and the glorious satisfaction of the harvest accomplished. That's how I learned that, to Mother, business had been the most effective tranquilizer against the loss of those she'd loved the most, and that since Ramón's death she had done nothing to show compassion to anyone. She hadn't done a single thing to show me, her daughter, the least bit of affection. Or my aunt and uncle, either. I learned that the only person to whom Mother would allow herself to feel a certain tenderness was Felisa, and that when she was finally sure of my old nanny's unconditional loyalty, she had decided to lock herself in the room and entrust herself to Felisa's care. Like a baby surrendering to its mother's hands. Like me surrendering to Angela because she was the only human being I had truly loved after Ramón. Uncle Cándido finished saying all that he had to say with a bite from a green apple, assuring me that Mother would rather set fire to her fifty stores scattered throughout forty cities than leave them in the hands of a stranger.

'All this gets me down as well. The responsibility torments me. I don't know what the problem is with me.' I had so little experience showing feelings in front of my family that I was about to burst into tears, unaware of how emotional I was.

'Your mother was a special case there. What do you want? To stay and end up like her?'

'I'm not like her.' A harsh voice emerged from within me. I was only trying to convince myself.

'Little Girl, like it or lump it, you're just like your mother.'

Uncle Cándido, seeing tears beginning to well that wanted to be kept entirely in his confidence, stroked the nape of my neck and I wept endlessly, because the direct link to my emotions was right there. The day turned gray and wonderful, much like a rainy night following a suffocatingly hot day. He offered me his chest and allowed to me to cry on it until I'd spent myself. He then pulled me away from his body, held my face in his hands, and looked into my eyes.

'Have you ever seen a bucket fall into a well after the rope?' I looked at him uncomprehendingly. 'It's only logical, Little Girl, that the rope should fall into the well after the bucket. But sometimes, sweetheart, things happen that have nothing to do with logic. Sign the document, go, and from wherever it is you're living, get in touch with the company that's running the business right now and act like the boss. When your mother dies, God forgive me, we'll sell it and no one' – here he continued to look deep into my eyes – 'no one, you hear?, is going to make us do what we don't want to. At least not here. What happens after that is up to you.'

I surrendered to his embrace once more, and he waited for my weeping to calm down to just a few sniffling sobs. He reminded me so much of Ramón that I let him guide me to the kitchen, allowed myself to be seated at the table, and held my face in my hands – Mother's customary gesture when she was desperate. To me, the bucket above the rope had become an inflated balloon rising in search of heaven.

'What would you like to eat? We have fish casserole, stuffed chicken, veal stew…'

'Fish casserole,' I replied, but whether I ate anything or not was all the same to me.

We reached Mother's apartment at nightfall. The windows were still open and the smell of waxed furniture dominated the space, draping it with a luxurious, queenly mantle. The first person we saw was Felisa, seated at the kitchen table, trying to polish silver knives, forks, and spoons that had never been used. Aunt Natalia was going from one place to another, looking for the right spot in which to set a vase brimming with orange lilies. I felt happy for the first time since I'd arrived, and I couldn't deny it. I kissed Felisa on the top of her hairdo and gave Aunt Natalia a hug. Behind me, Uncle Cándido returned to his usual self. He came in, went to say hello to Mother, and then sat in the living room to watch a football match. I understood that the same thing happened to Uncle Cándido as it did to me: that words such as happiness, pleasure, pride, illusion, ambition, emotion did not exist when he was at his sister's place. Everything we had discussed during the day disappeared like a happy dream upon waking. But I didn't care. I already knew what I had to do.

I went to see Mother, who in spite of being in bed was alarmingly vivacious, infected by Felisa and Natalia's euphoria. I informed her that I was going back to Mexico and would return during the Christmas holidays. It was hard for me to tell her, but I thought things would be smoother if she were the first to know.

'We'll continue with the letter when you return, because I don't know what to say now.' She had, however, become dejected.

'You don't know what to say to me, or you don't know what to say to Father?' I'd walked into the room with a couple of cigarettes and lit them while she thought. When she detected the smell of tobacco, she leapt like a champ over her sadness and reached out to accept the proffered cigarette.

'I just don't know what to say.'

'So don't say a word. Is the letter that important?'

She stuck a foot out from under the sheets and stared at it. She made a remark about how fast her toenails were growing and asked me to remember to trim them when she died. Even if I were in Mexico, I had to come back to trim her nails and perfume her. She also asked me not to forget to put socks on her feet, because death was very cold and empty.

'Is the letter so important, Mommy?'

'I started writing it for your father, but now I'm only thinking about Akiko. You know who Akiko is, don't you?'

I regarded her with a slow smile. I was so happy to have spoken with Uncle Cándido that it was easy for me to be compassionate. I even managed to feel the tenderness I was displaying toward her. I wasn't lying. She would have known if I'd been lying. She knew me better than

Angela did, and there was no way of misleading her.

'I know who Akiko is, Mommy. I've known it for many years.' I was again on the verge of letting her know that, the year before, Akiko had sent a Christmas card, because Father was surely, almost surely, dead. 'I know more than you think I know.'

She smoked slowly, and I opened the window to throw the cigarette butt into the hollow of the linden tree on the sidewalk.

'If you want to see if I can make the basket, get up.'

She smiled and said she'd take my word for it. I tried to make the basket, but the still burning cigarette fell into the empty flowerpot on the bottom floor. I don't know how, but she knew I'd missed. She even laughed, and I laughed too, with an open, unfettered, sincere laugh. With no deceit.

'You know what makes me sad?' she asked, looking at me from beyond everything we had experienced during the days I'd spent at her side. Looking at me from an acid sadness. 'I'm sad that I don't know anything about you.'

I thought about what Ramón had written in the *Anthology of Quotidian Objects* concerning coconuts: if the water doesn't flow, it means the coconut is rotten.

xxxxx

Read more fiction in English from Small Stations Press:

Miguel-Anxo Murado,
SOUNDCHECK: TALES FROM THE BALKAN CONFLICT

The death of a foreign cameraman outside
Karlovac, the threat of Serbian snipers in Zagreb,
a massacre of village peasants by guerrilla
fighters, a young Croat who joins forces with
a Serbian scrap merchant and is caught up in a
confrontation with Gypsies competing for scrap
metal left over by the war... The stories in
Miguel-Anxo Murado's *Soundcheck: Tales from the*
Balkan Conflict focus on the hostilities between
Croats and Serbs during the 1991 war in Croatia. Told with chilling
brevity and disarming intensity, the stories bring to life a conflict the
author himself covered as a foreign correspondent and are based
on real-life events or conversations that took place during the war.
Miguel-Anxo Murado, a regular contributor to *The New York Times*
and *The Guardian* newspapers, is known for his fiction based on his
experiences as a journalist in war-torn regions of the world, from the
ex-Yugoslavia to the Middle East. Inspired by fleeting conversations
or poignant scenes, he draws universal lessons about the nature and
ultimate destiny of humankind.

ISBN 978-954-384-037-3

Miguel-Anxo Murado, ASH WEDNESDAY

In this collection of sixteen short stories by the Galician writer Miguel-Anxo Murado, the reader is taken on a journey through the various rites of passage that make up an individual's life, from the months-old baby who lives in the eternal moment of Nothingness and quickly forgets an argument with his elder brother to the university professor who visits a colleague in Kyoto to see the cherry blossom and before the symbols of

impermanence is forced to confront his own terminal illness. Children and adults alike endure extreme situations, from a child who is bullied at school to the Chinese women workers who stay up all night to prepare a handmade suit for the morning. Sailors are rescued at sea; others are cast adrift when their ship sinks, at the mercy of the current. A young man is brought face to face with his late father when surrounded by a mountain blaze; a young girl endeavours to learn the secrets to her sister's radiant beauty. Two boys fall for the same girl; one tries to curry favour with the members of his gang in a story reminiscent of Isaac Babel's *Red Cavalry*, while another searches for the strength inside. All are caught in unexpected situations, elegantly and expertly described, and handed the task of how to react in a book that celebrates the human spirit across barriers of time and language.

ISBN 978-954-384-053-3

Xurxo Borrazás, **VICIOUS**

Shakespearean drama set in a Galician context. There is something strikingly postmodern – or Elizabethan – about this novel, in which a man from Laracha, south-west of Coruña, on Galicia's famed Coast of Death, is on the run for committing a multiple murder that shocks the local community and has the priest calling for the razing of the local slums. Chucho Monteiro, who has always been overlooked by his father in favor  of his younger brother, Daniel, more pliable, less violent, heads to the port of Coruña in order to effect his escape on the first ship weighing anchor, a ship that will take him not to Stratford, but to Southampton and on. In a fascinating, multi-layered narrative, the author keeps the reader guessing about the murderer's final destination until the very end. Narrative chronology is mixed up, and the veil between author and reader is torn in two, so that we're not sure if we are witnesses or partakers of this narrative. *Vicious* (called *Criminal* in Galician) is Xurxo Borrazás's second and best-known novel, and won him the Spanish Critics' Prize as well as the San Clemente Prize awarded by high-school readers.

ISBN 978-954-384-038-0

Ledicia Costas, AN ANIMAL CALLED MIST

In *An Animal Called Mist*, a book of six short stories, the Galician author Ledicia Costas (Winner of the 2015 Spanish National Book Award) walks the tightrope between fiction and reality in a superb and sometimes shocking narrative. She bases herself on real events in and after the Second World War – the Siege of Leningrad, the sinking of the USS *Indianapolis*, the dropping of atomic bombs on Hiroshima and

Nagasaki, the interrogation of Italian partisans by the Banda Koch, the sexual exploitation of women internees in Nazi concentration camps, the trials of high-ranking Nazi officials – and then recreates them, changing and inventing biographical details, giving free rein to her writer's imagination in order to produce a sequence of stories that look not so much at historical fact as at the essence of barbarism, the capacity of the human mind to conceive ways of torturing and tormenting fellow human beings. This is not a historical account of the Second World War – for that, the reader should consult works of history – but a book of fiction that focuses on the shadow projected by the events, their essence, the granulated content of their darkness. Ledicia Costas is one of Galicia's best-known writers who, in the tradition of writers such as Manuel Rivas and Agustín Fernández Paz, magnifies the voice of the persecuted in her narrative. *An Animal Called Mist* won the Losada Diéguez Prize for Literary Creation in 2016.

ISBN 978-954-384-062-5

Xabier P. DoCampo,
THE BOOK OF IMAGINARY JOURNEYS

Inspired by Italo Calvino's Invisible Cities, *The Book of Imaginary Journeys* by Xabier P. DoCampo follows in the tradition of great travel literature that began with Homer's Odyssey. It purports to be the transcription of two travel journals written by a certain X.B.R., in which the Traveller gives as objective a description as he can of the cities and kingdoms he visits. So it is he comes to a city you can only visit for three days or  where you cannot fall asleep, a city balanced on the fine point of a diamond or rotating on a water wheel, a city whose inhabitants are all tree-dwelling women or descended from birds, a city where the tombstones are inscribed not with the names of the deceased but with the titles of their favourite books, a city where money is only valid for a year, where none of its inhabitants can go fishing because all the rods have been turned into soldiers' lances, whose ministers are made to wear nooses as a warning to stay clean... The Traveller records songs, proverbs and remedies he hears along the way and describes some of the people he meets – a woman who conducts imaginary orchestras, a man who loves the earth so much he would like to plough it with a pair of unicorns, another searching for a treasure guarded by seven keys... Like translation, travel is a return to the source, the point of departure. What the Traveller takes away from the experience is what he has learned.

ISBN 978-954-384-063-2

For an up-to-date list of our publications, please visit
www.smallstations.com